RIPPLE EFFECT

OTHER BOOKS AND AUDIO BOOKS
BY TRACI HUNTER ABRAMSON:

Undercurrents

RIPPLE EFFECT

A NOVEL

TRACI HUNTER ABRAMSON

Covenant Communications, Inc.

Published by Covenant Communications, Inc.
American Fork, Utah

Printed in Canada
First Printing: February 2005

11 10 09 08 07 06 05   10 9 8 7 6 5 4 3 2 1

ISBN 1-59156-744-0

ACKNOWLEDGMENTS

My sincere thanks to Rebecca Cummings, Nikki Abramson, and Lynn Gardner for your invaluable help as the editing process began, and to Katie Child, Christian Sorensen, and Shauna Humphreys who helped me complete the challenge.

Thanks to David and LeNita Fitzgerald for sharing a glimpse of life in professional baseball, and to my sister Tiffany for having friends in every profession.

To my parents, thank you for believing that I could accomplish anything.

And a special thanks to my husband, Jonathan, for his continued support, and our children, Diana, Christina, Lara, and Luke, for sharing me with the computer.

PROLOGUE

Darkness closed in as she heard a movement behind her. She pushed forward, creeping through the night. Moonlight spilled down through the barren trees, leaves stirring beneath her feet. The woods were familiar, yet somehow she didn't know which way to go. Surely there must be a way out, a path to safety.

She pressed forward with a sense of urgency, her thoughts focused on escaping her pursuer. She saw the light in the distance, a lamp glowing in the window of the house that had been her safe haven for a time. Memories of those who dwelled inside turned her away from the warmth offered there. Instead she fled into the thick woods.

Underbrush tore at her clothes, scratched at her arms. She lifted one hand to protect her face from the branches that reached into the narrow path. A deer stood in a clearing ahead of her, its head held high. It stared at her for a moment before disappearing into the trees.

A twig snapped beneath her foot. She heard her own labored breathing, heard the rustle in the trees behind her, and made the mistake of turning and seeing the man who was still in pursuit. Her foot caught on a branch, and she stumbled to the cold ground. Fear consumed her and then paralyzed her.

She knew this man who now stood over her. She had even met and spoken with his wife. The distinguished Judge Christopher Rush, the man responsible for Chase's murder, stared down at her with dark, heartless eyes. His face was expressionless as he lifted the gun and pointed it at her.

The wind screamed, masking any sound that might have come from her. Even as she accepted her fate, a sound behind him made the judge turn, swinging the gun toward the movement as Matt stepped from the trees.

"No!" Kylie sat up straight in bed, her breathing still labored. She looked around in the darkness, surprised to find herself safe in her apartment. Pressing a hand to her pounding heart, she closed her eyes against the horrible sight that had just flashed through her mind.

"It's not real," Kylie whispered to herself, trying not to remember how real the scene could have been just the year before.

She opened her eyes again and looked around her room. This was real now. She was Kylie Ramsey, student, swimmer. Chase, the first man she had ever loved, was gone. Taken too soon from this life by the evil that continued to haunt her. The fact that Chase had been murdered after uncovering information about the smuggling ring he was investigating should have been a bad dream instead of reality.

Her eyes filled with tears as she remembered Chase standing next to her at her father's funeral, just a month before his own untimely death. An immense part of her world had dropped away after the death of her father, the incredible man who'd raised her after her mother died so young, and she found herself alone, orphaned, with only Chase by her side. When Chase was killed, what was left of her world turned completely upside down.

The same evil that had taken Chase now kept her from Matt Whitmore, the man who held such a large piece of her heart. Matt had penetrated the shield around her heart, teaching her how to live again, how to love again. He had promised to wait for her. Yet how could she know if she would ever be truly safe? And was her own happiness worth risking Matt's safety?

Her heart heavy, Kylie stepped from her bed and crossed to the window. She looked out into the darkness, knowing that, despite her many prayers, she still didn't have the answers.

CHAPTER 1

Matt lifted a hand as he drove past several teammates walking through the parking lot of the baseball stadium. He pulled out of the nearly empty lot, past the strip of sports bars, gas stations, and fast-food restaurants. He glanced at the apartments many of the other baseball players lived in during the season. The stucco on some of the outside walls was cracked, and he had heard some of his teammates complain about the size of the apartments. Not for the first time, Matt was grateful that his parents had provided him with the means to get started out in life.

His mother had insisted that if he was going to be living on the road as often as not, he needed to have some place that would feel like home. Since he had managed to graduate a semester early from college, the funds set aside for that last semester were now going to help him set up house here in Texas.

The apartment he rented was nearly fifteen minutes from the stadium, a distance he considered extremely reasonable after growing up in northern Virginia just outside of Washington, D.C. Thankfully, his manager decided to have spring training at their home stadium. He doubted he would have wanted to spend the first eight weeks of the season living out of a hotel room.

When he was halfway to his apartment, a fender bender slowed traffic to a crawl for nearly a mile. Matt simply turned the music up, glad that he had already taken the time to program the local stations into his car radio. He gave a passing thought to stopping by the grocery store but quickly rejected it as fatigue overtook him.

By the time he unlocked his apartment door, his muscles were aching from overuse. His duffel bag dropped to the floor with a resounding thud. A baseball freed itself from the bag, rolling across the ceramic-tile floor. Matt collapsed on his couch, oblivious to the dried mud he had tracked through the apartment.

He rested his eyes, stretching his full six-foot-three frame, hoping he could will away the tightness in his shoulders. As his stomach growled, he wished once again that his phone was hooked up. "Two more days," he muttered. Until then, he had to rely on himself rather than the pizza deliveryman for meals.

With a groan, he stood and crossed the room to the refrigerator. He opened it, hoping that food had miraculously appeared while he was gone. It was still empty. He rifled through the few items in his cabinets, wondering if he could make something out of a half jar of peanut butter, a package of trail mix, and a can of tuna.

"Shaye would be able to make something with this." Matt held up the can of tuna and shook his head in frustration. He hadn't seen her in over a year, yet he could still remember their last moments together like it was yesterday.

Her hair had been dry for once as they said good-bye at the bed and breakfast in Vermont. His family and numerous government agents waited outside as Matt held her close that last time. Even now, he could imagine the smell of her hair, the softness of her skin, and the fear in her eyes.

He knew Shaye was dead now, even though her body and mind lived on. Her life as Shaye Kendall had ceased to exist the minute Matt had been shot by the man sent to kill her. Her testimony was vital to closing down one of the largest smuggling operations ever uncovered, and until it was over, her life would continue to be at risk.

She was still out there somewhere, with a new name and a new past. What he wouldn't give to know the name of the only woman he had ever loved.

The knock on the door caused Matt to push aside his hunger for the moment. He opened it to find two girls about his age. The curvy blonde posed in the doorway, shaking her thick mane behind her shoulders. Her appraisal of his appearance was anything but subtle as she studied his handsome, all-American face, broad shoulders, and athletic build. Her eyes sparked with interest as she brought her gaze back to his face, strong features framed by blond hair that was in need of a trim.

Uncomfortable with the blonde's obvious assessment, Matt turned to the redhead, who was smiling warmly. In her hands she held a loaf of bread wrapped in plastic.

"We came to welcome you to our ward." The redhead shifted the bread into his hands. "I'm Caitlin Warner, and this is Leslie Anderson."

"Thanks." Matt took a deep breath, inhaling the homey scent. "You may have just saved me from starvation."

"You haven't had dinner yet?" Leslie asked hopefully.

Matt shook his head. "I was just considering my options."

"You know, you're welcome to come eat with us," Leslie suggested. "Our family home evening group is coming over after dinner, and you could meet some of the other young single adults in our ward."

"I wouldn't want to impose." Matt shook his head even as his stomach grumbled in protest.

"You wouldn't be imposing," Caitlin said. "Veronica is cooking, and she always makes enough for a week's worth of dinners."

"Are you sure?" Matt hesitated.

"Come on." Leslie reached for his hand and pulled him outside. "I'll ride with you and show you the way."

Matt freed his hand and held up the bread. "Let me just put this inside." When he walked back outside, Matt stepped beside Caitlin. "I'll just follow you."

Caitlin nodded. "We only live a few blocks away."

Leslie's lips formed a small pout, but before she could protest, Matt was already halfway to his car.

When they arrived at the girls' apartment, the scent of tomato sauce drifted through the air. Caitlin opened the door to reveal a tidy apartment decorated with a number of homemade projects. The pillows on the couch were embroidered in every color imaginable, and various knickknacks and wall hangings were in different stages of completion.

"Veronica! We brought one more for dinner," Caitlin called into the kitchen.

A tiny, olive-skinned girl poked her head out. Her black hair was pulled back into a ponytail, and she had to stretch to stand five foot two. "Hi, I'm Veronica. You must be the new guy in the ward."

Matt nodded, shaking her outstretched hand. "Matt Whitmore."

"Dinner's almost ready." Veronica motioned them to the table as she retreated to the kitchen.

When she walked back out holding a pan of lasagna, Matt thought he had died and gone to heaven. "Oh, wow!"

Caitlin laughed, shaking her head. "Is it true that the way to a man's heart is through his stomach?"

"I think I heard that somewhere," Matt managed as his thoughts turned to the woman who had already claimed his heart. Shaye could certainly hold her own in the kitchen, but his heart had been lost to her long before he had discovered her culinary talents. He averted his eyes a moment until he was sure his emotions were no longer evident there.

After Matt offered a blessing on the food, he was sure he was as close to heaven as he could get under the circumstances. "Veronica, where did you learn to cook like this?"

"My father owns an Italian restaurant. All of the family worked in it at one time or another." Veronica served herself another piece. Matt grinned when she automatically placed another piece on his plate as well.

Shortly after they ate, the other members of their family home evening group arrived. Matt chatted with the new arrivals, instinctively offering only superficial answers to their questions about him. As the evening settled down and Leslie gradually slid closer to Matt on the couch, Matt finally stood and excused himself to go home.

Veronica earned Matt's undying gratitude when she not only sent some leftovers with him but also intercepted Leslie as she tried to walk him out to his car. Veronica just rolled her eyes as Leslie started to pout when Matt made his getaway.

Matt sighed as he carefully placed the plate of food on the front seat of his car. Girls like Leslie had been too much a part of his life before he met Shaye. During high school, Matt rarely had to ask girls out because they always asked him first. The combination of his baseball abilities and the fact that his father was a U.S. senator had given him a healthy share of dates. His classic good looks and easygoing personality had put him over the top in popularity.

As much as he loved his dad, he hoped the senator's shadow didn't reach as far as this small Texas suburb. His decision to play professional baseball had been a difficult one. Though he was talented at and loved the game, he knew that success would only put him more in the public eye. And that was the one place Shaye didn't want to be.

CHAPTER 2

"Kylie, you have to help us," Jill insisted, hoping that being four years older than her roommates would add some extra influence. She looked to Brooke, their other roommate, for reinforcement.

"She's right," Brooke agreed. "You hardly ever do anything with our young single adults group. We're starting to think that you don't like men."

"I don't have good luck when it comes to the opposite sex." Kylie raked her fingers through her dark brown hair. Her roommates had been after her for the better part of a year to start dating. They didn't seem to be deterred by the fact that the only single man in the family ward they attended was sixty-three years old.

"Look, all we need you to do is make sure we have a lifeguard. We'll take care of everything else," Jill promised.

"Do you really think everyone will want to go swimming?" Kylie asked skeptically. She held up the flyer announcing next week's young single adult activity—a swimming party. "I mean, it's the day before Valentine's Day. I thought you would have a dance or something like that."

"Nobody wants to go to a dance unless they have a date. Last year we had one, and the turnout was lousy. Hopefully, this will be something fun for everyone." Brooke pulled a gallon tub of ice cream from the church's freezer and handed it to Kylie. "Besides, it's not like we're going to make everyone get their hair wet."

"How did we get roped into helping you tonight?" Kylie wrestled the container open and started scooping out the ice cream.

"Because you still remember what it was like to be a young woman," Brooke told her. Brooke had been the Mia Maid advisor for three weeks, and her two roommates felt like they had been extended the calling as well.

"As long as we don't have to chaperone any slumber parties." Jill cringed at the thought. Just because she taught second grade didn't mean she wanted a bunch of fourteen-year-olds invading their apartment. She rather liked having her own bedroom since returning from her mission. She knew Brooke too well to think that she and Kylie wouldn't get dragged into joining the slumber party too.

"Now there's an idea." Brooke grinned mischievously.

Kylie lifted the ice cream scoop and handed it to Jill. "Hate to scoop and run, but I've got to go." She licked the ice cream off her fingers before adding, "Jill, don't let her get carried away."

"Who, me?" Brooke almost succeeded in looking innocent. Only the sparkle in her deep green eyes gave her away.

"We're going grocery shopping on our way home. Do you want us to get you anything?" Jill asked.

Kylie opened her mouth, but before she could answer, Brooke said, "Besides muffins and juice."

Kylie just laughed. "Not that I can think of."

"You'd think she'd get tired of having the same thing for breakfast every day." Brooke shook her head.

Kylie unzipped her swim bag and pulled out a banana nut muffin. "They make a good snack too." She pushed the kitchen door open, pulling the hood of her sweatshirt up to block out the February chill. She hesitated in the doorway just long enough to scan the dark parking lot before forcing herself to continue outside. "See you later."

* * *

Matt pulled into the parking lot, sizing up the building where he would now be attending church. The church looked very much like the one where he had attended meetings growing up, except instead of being set among the greenery of Virginia, this church was perched up on a small hill overlooking miles of wide-open spaces.

The moon was already visible even though the last of the sun's rays were still lingering on the horizon. Matt took a moment to appreciate the splendor of the land and the contrast of the dusk against the tidy neighborhoods below. Once, he would have felt compelled to re-create this beauty in his sketch pad or on a canvas. That was before.

As he climbed out of his car, he glanced at a girl leaving from the far end of the building. Suddenly he was transported back in time. The girl could have been Shaye the first time he saw her, wearing shorts in the middle of winter with a hooded sweatshirt hiding her face. Matt took a step toward the girl before he stopped himself.

Of course it couldn't be her. Still, he watched her cross to her car, her fluid movements not unlike Shaye's. He tried to put Shaye out of his mind but knew that it was impossible. Even now, after more than a year, it was her face that formed in his mind when he found himself daydreaming. Too frequently, he still awoke at night from the memory of her scent. Shaking his head to clear the memories, he forced himself to walk toward the building, and the emptiness returned.

A group of deacons charged out the door before Matt could enter. He waded through the boys and made his way to the gym. The volleyball net was already set up, and several people he had met at family home evening earlier that week were dividing up into teams. Matt let out a sigh of relief when he noticed Leslie was not among them.

"Hey, Matt." Caitlin waved for him to join them. "Glad you could make it."

"He's on my team," Veronica claimed.

"No way. You always get the tall players." Caitlin settled her hands on her hips.

"I need someone to make up for my shortness." Veronica grabbed Matt's arm and pulled him to her side of the net. Lowering her voice, she asked, "You can play, can't you?"

"If I say no, are you going to throw me back?" Matt laughed.

"Be nice, or I won't cook for you again," Veronica threatened.

Matt held up his hands in a gesture of peace. "Okay, okay. I can play."

A group of young women raced through the far end of the gym as they were starting their game. Matt nodded at them and asked, "What's going on here tonight?"

"Some youth activity for the other ward."

Before the door closed all the way, one of the leaders came in and walked over to the game. "Veronica, can I give these to you?"

"Sure, Brooke. What are they?" Veronica took the papers from her, reading over the flyer.

"Our next young single adult activity is a swimming party. A week from Friday." Brooke glanced from Veronica to Matt. "You must be new. I'm Brooke Sutherland."

"Matt Whitmore."

"Matt just moved into our ward a few days ago," Veronica offered.

"I hope you can come next week," Brooke said before following another group of young women out of the gym.

* * *

Matt walked onto the pool deck, surveying the team practicing in the water. He knew he was crazy for even being here, but since seeing that girl at the church, he had been haunted by memories.

The swimmers in the pool were difficult to distinguish from one another. Matt watched them carefully, looking for the familiar power and grace in the water. He quickly determined that none of these swimmers were in the same league as Shaye. Shaking his head, he scolded himself for thinking she might even be in the same state as he, much less the same town. He still hoped for her sake that the FBI could help her keep her Olympic dreams alive.

After witnessing her boyfriend's murder, Shaye had been placed in protective custody, where Matt had met and fallen in love with her. Her safety had been jeopardized because of her association with his family, forcing her to give up that identity and move on to a new one. Matt held tight to the hope that she would want to find him again once the trial was over.

The trial of Chris Rush, the man who wanted her dead, had been scheduled several times, but his lawyers had successfully delayed it over and over again. If everything went as planned, she would be able to return to her true identity of Christal Jones once Rush was convicted.

As the swim practice ended, Matt continued to watch as the goggles and caps came off and the swimmers reclaimed their identities. A sigh of frustration escaped him. How many times had he tried to find her in a crowd, or stopped by a swim practice, or picked up the phone hoping to hear her voice? Almost as many times as he had imagined holding her again.

Walking toward the parking lot, Matt heard his name being called. His hopes soared for a moment, but when he looked around, he only saw Brooke, the girl he had met at volleyball the night before.

"Do you go to school here?" Brooke asked as she caught up with him.

Matt shook his head. "I was just checking out the facilities."

"This is where we're having our swimming party next week," Brooke told him. "Are you going to come?"

"Probably."

"Good. I'm worried that we won't have a big turnout. The guy who was supposed to make our posters flaked on us." Brooke shrugged.

"A lot of people got the flyers you were handing out."

"Yeah, but most of the people who come to these activities work in the evenings and only get to church on Sundays. It's hard to get flyers to everyone."

"If you have the materials, I could make some posters for you," Matt offered.

"Really?" Brooke's eyes lit up. "I mean, we tried to make some, but I'm not very artistic, and neither are my roommates."

"It shouldn't take very long, especially if you and your roommates could help with the lettering after I draw them," Matt told her.

"Are you free tonight?" Brooke asked hopefully. "If you want, you can come over for dinner, and we could work on them afterward."

The beginnings of a smile tugged at his mouth. "I never refuse a home-cooked meal."

"Great." Brooke wrote down her address and handed it to him. "How about six o'clock?"

"I'll see you then." He tucked Brooke's address in his pocket and headed to his car.

Matt arrived at Brooke's apartment a few minutes after six. He caught his breath when a tall blonde answered the door. Her hair was cropped short, and she looked like she had just stepped off the cover of a magazine.

"You must be Matt." She opened the door and welcomed him inside. "I'm Jill, Brooke's roommate."

Brooke came rushing into the living room as Matt entered. "Oh, I'm so glad you made it!"

Matt nodded, surveying the room. The contemporary furniture had a southwestern flavor. Native American rugs adorned the floor and the walls, and the room was warmed by framed photographs.

"I like your apartment." Matt stepped closer to the photos on the wall, seeing each of the girls included in a family photo. "Just the two of you live here?"

"No. Our other roommate went to work out." Jill told him. "Why don't we eat first, and then we can work on the posters."

Matt and Brooke nodded in agreement.

After the table was cleared, Brooke spread out some poster board and markers.

"Do you have a pencil?" Matt asked, squaring a piece of poster board in front of him.

"Yeah." Jill opened a kitchen drawer and handed him a pencil along with one of the flyers they had been handing out. "All of the information should be on this."

With pencil in hand, Matt read over the information. Using the technique he had learned in his art classes, he began putting lines on the poster board until finally he handed the completed drawing to Brooke. "How's this?"

"This is great!" Brooke looked at the sketch. A huge wave dominated the page, and Matt had sketched a guy and a girl surfing on top of it. "We could write 'Catch the Wave' on the top here."

"And then put all of the information on the bottom," Jill agreed enthusiastically.

For the next two hours, they created one poster after another. Finally, Matt pushed back from the table. "I had better get going."

"Thanks so much for your help," Brooke told him. "These will really help us get the word out."

"No problem. Thanks for dinner." Matt walked outside into the cool night air, hesitating when he was halfway across the parking lot. He looked around, as though searching for something familiar.

Dismissively, he shook his head and climbed into his car. As he drove into the night, again he had the urge to look behind him. He slowed, still not seeing anything unusual. "I must be more tired than

I thought," he muttered to himself as he sped up and headed toward his apartment.

* * *

She stopped short of her apartment door, sensing something from the past, but she didn't know what. Kylie unlocked the door with a last glance behind her. When she stepped inside, she stopped suddenly.

The fragrance was faint, but all too familiar. She took a deep breath, and memories came rushing back. Kylie had never told her roommates about the man she loved. That part of her heart had been locked up for more than a year. Only when she was alone did she unlock the memories and hope for the chance to make more.

"Kylie, come look at these," Brooke called from the kitchen.

With a shake of her head, Kylie forced herself back to the present. She entered the kitchen and found both of her roommates looking over posters. "I thought you weren't going to do posters."

"A new guy from the other ward came over and helped us out," Jill told her.

"It's amazing what guys will do for a meal." Brooke laughed.

A smiled played on Kylie's mouth as she nodded in agreement. She leaned over the table and looked at the posters, recognizing the skill it had required to create them. The style was very much like many of Matt's sketches. With a shake of her head, she tried to clear his image from her mind. "These are really good."

"Hopefully now we'll have a decent turnout." Brooke smiled as she shuffled the posters for Kylie to see.

"Is everything all set for us to use the pool?" Jill asked.

"Yeah. We just have to make sure everyone cleans up after themselves because we'll be the last ones there." Kylie moved into the kitchen and opened the refrigerator. "Did you guys save me any dinner?"

"It's on the bottom shelf," Jill told her.

Kylie opened the plastic container and popped it into the microwave. "You haven't told me about your artist."

"Tall, blond, handsome . . ." Jill started.

"And taken," Brooke added.

"We don't know that," Jill insisted.

Brooke looked at Jill and then at Kylie. "He didn't even hint at wanting to take Jill out. He's obviously already off the market."

"Oh, please," Jill sighed and shook her head. "You act like every guy I meet asks me out."

"Name the last one who didn't," Brooke challenged.

"Matt."

All of the color drained out of Kylie's face as she felt her knees go weak. To steady herself, she grabbed the kitchen counter, allowing the edges to dig into the palms of her hands.

"Are you okay?" Concerned, Jill hurried into the kitchen.

Kylie forced herself to straighten. She took a deep breath, trying to regain her composure. "I just need to eat something."

Jill nodded toward the table. "You go sit down. I'll fix your plate for you."

"Thanks." Kylie made her way to the table and sat by Brooke. She looked at the posters in a new light, studying them for a familiar style. Lots of guys named Matt knew how to draw, didn't they? Shaking her head, she convinced herself she was just dreaming the impossible again.

CHAPTER 3

Matt arrived at the swimming party right on time, which was fifteen minutes early by Mormon Standard Time. He was surprised to walk inside and find a good number of people already there.

Inside the pool area, girls in swimming suits clustered around the deck, and only a few guys had actually gotten into the pool. Catching a glimpse of Leslie posing on a lounge chair, Matt smiled to himself at the thought of seeing her with wet hair. He had gotten used to seeing Shaye fresh out of the pool, but girls like Leslie took care to keep their hair dry and their makeup on.

He never realized how much he would miss such simple things about Shaye. Yet since they had been apart, he had come to truly appreciate the way she was so genuine and unassuming. He even missed the way she could go from being self-assured to vulnerable in the blink of an eye.

Leslie looked up and saw him, and Matt automatically averted his eyes. That's when he saw her. His heart skipped a beat as he stepped closer to the pool.

The girl swimming in the far lane glided effortlessly through the water with barely a splash. He stared, waiting, hoping. He didn't realize he was holding his breath until Jill touched his arm.

"She's amazing, isn't she?" Jill beamed with pride.

"You know her?" Matt asked, hoping he sounded casual.

"I live with her." Jill laughed. "She's my other roommate."

"She's really good." He tried not to wince at his own understatement.

"Yeah. We all think she'll be in the Olympics some day, but she doesn't believe us."

Matt just nodded, watching her finally come to a stop at the far end of the pool. She stripped off her cap and goggles, revealing her medium-length brown hair. As she leaned back and smoothed her hair, Matt's heart leaped into his throat.

"Shaye." The word escaped him, barely a whisper.

"What?" Jill looked at him, confused.

"Uh, she should listen to you." Matt tried to recover. "She probably will be in the Olympics some day."

When he looked back to the pool, she was gone. Had it really been her? He questioned his eyesight as well as his sanity for a moment. His heart was still racing as Jill began introducing him to some people from her ward. He could hardly keep his attention focused on the people in front of him as the reality of the situation hit him. Could he really have moved to the same town his girlfriend had been relocated to? The odds of them finding each other by chance were worse than winning the lottery, yet here they were in the same building. And on the day before Valentine's Day, no less.

He could just hear what Doug would say when he found out. *If* he found out. Doug Valdez had been one of the FBI agents who helped protect Shaye during her first relocation. Matt guessed that he was still on her case, especially since he had easily stepped into the role of her boyfriend when the need arose.

Matt tried to position himself so he could see the locker room door, but as soon as Jill moved away to welcome some newcomers, Leslie appeared at his side.

"I see you've been meeting everyone." She stepped closer, possessively hooking her arm through Matt's.

Matt nodded, looking around for someone to rescue him. Unless he yanked his arm away, Leslie wasn't likely to let go. "Looks like you have a good singles group here."

"Oh, we do, especially in our ward," Leslie agreed halfheartedly. "Most of the singles in the other wards are still in college."

"And our ward?" Matt asked. The people he had met so far also appeared to be in their early to mid-twenties.

"Most of us are the young professional type."

"Really?" Matt took a step away from Leslie, hoping to break her death grip on his arm. "Are you a young professional?"

"I'm a model," Leslie purred.

"How fascinating." He noticed Jill nearby, hoping desperately she would help him out.

"It is," Leslie agreed. "What do you do?"

"Oh, nothing as exciting as modeling." Matt caught Jill's eye and tried to hide his relief when she joined them.

"Hi, Leslie." Jill smiled warmly. "I hope you don't mind, but I need to steal Matt away from you for just a minute."

Leslie's eyes narrowed, and her grip on Matt's arm tightened. "Oh, really?"

"We need him to help us move the lifeguard stand." Jill looked at Matt hopefully.

"I'm sure someone else . . ."

"I forgot I had promised to do that for you." Matt freed himself from Leslie and stepped back. "I'll see you later."

He followed Jill to the far lifeguard stand. "I owe you. Big-time."

"After all the work you did on those posters, we'll consider us even." Jill laughed.

"Do you really need this moved?" Matt asked.

"No, but Leslie will notice if we don't." Jill grabbed one end and helped Matt move it back from the pool. "That looks good."

"Now, how do I avoid Leslie for the rest of the night?" Matt asked.

"Take my advice." Jill gave him a playful push toward the pool. "Get in the water."

Matt stepped backward and lost his balance. Jill grabbed his hand to keep him from falling, but instead she fell in right behind him.

Jill sputtered water as she came back to the surface. "I can't believe you pulled me in!"

"It wasn't intentional," Matt told her, only stretching the truth a little. "I hope you hadn't planned to keep your hair dry."

"Very funny," Jill laughed, swimming over to the side. She decided since she was already wet, she would find others to join her.

Matt took off his soaking T-shirt and tossed it onto the deck. He watched Jill in action, cajoling her friends into coming in the pool. When someone jumped in behind him, he turned. His eyes quickly shifted from the guy who had caused the splash to the girl on the deck.

A smile played on his lips as their eyes met and held. Time froze, and for a moment, everyone else faded into the background. No one existed but the two of them as he watched the expression on her face change from shock to disbelief to amazement. His heart pounded as he recognized the hope dawning in her eyes.

The moment was short-lived, interrupted by a group trying to start up a game of water polo. When Matt looked back to her, he was disappointed to see her walking away with Brooke.

Everything in him wanted to jump out of the pool, pull her into his arms, and make her promise that she would stay with him forever. Reality demanded that he pretend he didn't know her. Even though fate had brought them back together again, to the world they were strangers. In fact, he didn't even know her new name.

* * *

Kylie followed Brooke to help arrange the refreshments. Brooke knew her roommate well enough to know that she used the pool for one thing, and if there wasn't room for her to swim laps, then she might as well not be in it.

Kylie could only hope that Brooke didn't notice her heart hammering in her chest as she tried to keep her focus away from the pool.

"I hope we have enough." Brooke glanced over the platters of cookies. Sugar cookies shaped like hearts were frosted with pink and white icing. Other platters contained the more traditional chocolate chip cookies. Brooke meticulously arranged them once again.

"How many pizzas did you order?" Kylie asked, trying to keep her voice normal as she ached to stare at Matt. What was he doing here? Had he followed her here, or was it just a coincidence that he had shown up? And had he found someone else during the past year? Kylie forced herself to turn her attention back to her roommate.

"Twenty." Brooke surveyed the crowd. "Do you think that's enough?"

"Relax, Brooke. It'll be fine." Kylie forced a smile. "Go swim for a while. I'll keep an eye on things here."

"Are you sure?" Brooke hesitated, torn between the fun in the pool and her sense of obligation.

"I can handle it," Kylie promised.

"Okay, okay." Brooke stepped toward the pool. "Just yell if you need me."

Kylie nodded, glancing at the game of water polo. Matt stood out even from this distance. His height had him towering over many of the people in the pool, and the ends of his blond hair curled slightly, indicating he was past due for a haircut. She didn't need to observe the women on deck to know that Matt was already causing heads to turn. Her quick glimpse had already taken in his well-toned arms, indicating he was still working out in some manner. Beyond his magnetic smile and exceptional good looks, he exuded an air of confidence and a sense of humor that naturally drew people to him. She sighed, wistfully reminding herself that in her last life, he had been her closest friend.

As she watched him play in the water, her mind turned to the time they had spent together that first semester of her freshman year. They had started out as friends and then became so much more. Even before he knew her deepest secrets, Matt had always been there for her. He had become her best friend. Kylie's thoughts were interrupted when the pizza deliveryman arrived.

The scent of pizza filled the air, and the pool cleared quickly. Kylie saw Matt coming toward her with the crowd. She wanted desperately to talk to him, to be close to him, but her memories already had her eyes tearing. The same sense of panic she had felt when she had last dreamed of Chris Rush seized her once again. She had been living under this identity for over a year, and yet now, with so many people around, she didn't trust herself to maintain it. As Matt approached, Kylie's eyes met his, and she offered him a smile before turning and escaping into the locker room.

She had barely walked in when Leslie and Caitlin entered the locker room.

"Can you believe how everyone is just falling all over him?" Leslie whined. "He hardly even had a chance to talk to me before he got pushed into the pool."

"He isn't a prize to be won." Caitlin's voice was patient as they walked farther inside to where Kylie was sitting. "Hi, Kylie. Are you okay?"

"I just wanted to wait for the crowd to die down before I went for some pizza," Kylie managed to say.

"At least Kylie is showing a little class." Leslie flipped her hair as she nodded toward her. "I think you're the only girl here who hasn't thrown herself at Matt."

"Matt?" Kylie asked, feigning ignorance. Her mind wandered back to that moment she saw him in the pool. If only she could find a way to talk with him for a few minutes. Could she risk it? Being away from him for so long had been difficult, but pretending she didn't know him when he was so close was pure torture.

"The new guy in our ward."

"I don't think I've met him yet." Kylie shrugged a shoulder, drawing on all of her strength to lie convincingly. "But his name sounds familiar. I think he's the one who helped Jill and Brooke draw the posters for tonight."

"Jill was following him around earlier," Leslie said, disgusted.

"I doubt that." Kylie stiffened as she instinctively defended Jill. "Besides, I got the impression that he already has a girlfriend."

Leslie's face turned red as she demanded, "Who told you that?"

"My roommates said something about it." Kylie shrugged, hoping she sounded casual. "Of course, they could have been mistaken, but they said he acted like he was already involved with someone."

"Maybe that explains why he hasn't asked you out," Caitlin suggested, trying to soothe Leslie's obviously wounded ego.

"We'll just see about that," Leslie huffed. "If I can ever get him alone, I'll just ask him straight out and see what he says."

"I don't know if that's such a good idea," Caitlin warned. "You might scare him off."

"He does look like the kind of guy who likes to do the asking," Kylie agreed.

"What would you know about it?" Leslie turned on Kylie. "You never date anyway."

Kylie just shrugged. "You're right, Leslie. I'm certainly no expert." Kylie turned to Caitlin. "I think I'll go see if there's any pizza left."

As Kylie walked out, she heard Caitlin scolding Leslie for being rude. Shaking her head, Kylie hoped that Matt had gotten his fill of Barbie-doll types before he had met Shaye.

CHAPTER 4

"One, two, three, four, five . . ." Kylie counted to herself, rotating her body in the water onto her other side. She continued to kick on her side as she performed the backstroke drill again. Passing under the flags, Kylie flipped over onto her stomach and executed a flip turn, powering off the wall on her back as she used the dolphin kick to propel herself.

She tried to concentrate on her body position as she cut through the water, but her mind wouldn't cooperate. How could she concentrate when just three days before, Matt had been here, swimming in this very pool? She didn't know why he was here, but from what Leslie and Caitlin had said, it sounded like he was living in town. If there had been a singles ward nearby, she might have been able to see him at church each week and hear the latest gossip about "the new guy," as he was currently being called. Instead, she could only hope to get tidbits of information through the network of single adults that her roommates often socialized with.

Surely Matt couldn't have moved to Texas without somehow knowing she was living here, yet Doug hadn't said anything about it the last time she spoke to him. She had even checked her cell phone for messages from Doug when she had gotten home from the swimming party only to find that he hadn't called her.

Her stomach knotted with anticipation as she wondered when she might see Matt again. Then her mind clouded with memories of those first weeks they spent together as their friendship bloomed and then grew to be something more. In Virginia, Matt would have come inside to watch the last few minutes of practice. Then they would have eaten breakfast together, spending that hour each morning talking about everything or about nothing in particular.

Kylie executed another turn, stopping suddenly when her hand rammed into the swimmer in front of her. Turning onto her stomach, she stroked freestyle as she passed one of her training partners, another Olympic hopeful.

When she reached the other end of the pool, Ryan stopped her. He had been her private coach for more than a year, and Kylie found he was far more demanding than anyone who had coached her previously. "Kylie, you still need to rotate your shoulders more." He lifted one arm high above his head, going through the motions for her, instructing her as he did so. "Remember that you're reaching for the still water beneath you."

Kylie nodded, wondering if she would ever master the backstroke, her weakest of the four competitive strokes. "Are you sure I have a shot in the IM?"

"The individual medley is by far your best chance at a medal," Ryan told her. "You have a great shot at the breaststroke leg of the medley relay too, but I don't want you to rely on just that one stroke to carry you to the Olympics."

Kylie floated back in the water. "Again?"

"Again." Ryan motioned for her to start, watching as Kylie began her next set of drills. Two more times he stopped her, trying to perfect her stroke.

She tried to bury her frustration as she focused on improving her backstroke, despite years of avoiding it in both practice and competition. Knowing that five other swimmers in the pool also hoped to compete in the Olympics made Kylie wonder if she would ever make it that far. So many people had the dream, yet so few ever achieved it. As Ryan continued to make demands, Kylie struggled to concentrate on his instructions.

Only when Kylie neared the end of practice and began her cooldown did she let her mind wander once again to Matt. She had thought of him often during the past few days, even looking for him at church on Sunday. Her stomach turned to a bundle of nerves every time she thought of seeing him again, wondering if they would finally speak.

She tried to push aside her insecurities as she thought of the girls who had vied for his attention at the swimming party. Leslie had not been the only girl trying to stake a claim on the new guy in town. The fact that Matt's good looks were attracting so much female attention annoyed her. More, she admitted to herself, she was annoyed that so many people were judging him based on his looks and not taking the time to appreciate his open, friendly nature and the way he saw the beauty in everything around him.

Even her own roommates had brought his name up a few times, but at least their comments had included an appreciation of his sense of humor. Besides, she knew she could trust them to wait for a guy to ask them out. They both already had a fair share of dates anyway, and everyone was betting that Brooke would end up married to the missionary she had sent off almost a year before, even though he insisted she date while he was gone.

Kylie had tried to imagine that Matt was on a mission and that she was just waiting for him to return. Uncertainty crowded her mind as she reminded herself that they had been apart for more than a year, and he might have started dating someone else. She tried to push the doubts aside, instead thinking of the way Matt had been so reluctant to say good-bye before she moved to Texas.

The transition to this identity had not been as difficult as she had expected. The loneliness could still creep up on her at unexpected times, but her life had become increasingly normal as time went on. After living in relative safety for more than a year, the memories of being chased by her old boyfriend's killers had dimmed. Only her decision to study criminal procedure in school continued to remind her of the violence in her past. But while her fears for her own safety had diminished over time, her concerns for Matt's safety had increased.

The remembrance of how he had fought with the man sent to kill her still gave her far too many bad dreams at night. Matt had been fortunate that when the gun discharged, the bullet had only grazed his leg, not causing any permanent damage. Still, the sight of him lying on the ground bleeding had made her face the fact that she was a dangerous person to be around. It could happen again, Kylie knew. He had protected her and was wounded in the process. How could she be sure that he would walk away whole the next time Chris Rush sent someone after her?

Until the trial was over, she knew she and Matt wouldn't truly be free to be together. Even as doubts crowded her mind, she tried to convince herself that the love she and Matt had found was strong enough to survive the time and distance.

* * *

Whack. Matt connected with the baseball, sending it flying over the left field fence. He resumed his stance to prepare for the next pitch of batting practice. This one he sent through the hole over second base. After passing on the next pitch, Matt connected once again for his second home run of the afternoon.

His frustration had continued to mount since seeing Shaye at the swimming party. He had never known he could be so happy and so frustrated about a single event. On one hand, he was thrilled to see her again and to find himself close to her. But on the other hand, he hadn't even been able to speak to her yet.

When he had been introduced to others at the party, she had never been nearby. He had seen her retreat into the locker room at one point, and worry gnawed at his stomach. How was she? Were Chris Rush's men still searching for her by following him? And had she found someone else while they were apart?

He tried to push that thought aside as he abused another base-ball, sending it along the third-base line. Doug Valdez had encouraged both of them to start dating others. He pointed out that if Matt dated, the men hunting for Shaye would be less likely to watch him. Hopefully, Rush's men might even believe the story about her being killed and stop looking for her altogether. On Shaye's end, dating would just help her look like a typical twenty-year-old.

What Doug didn't understand was the way singles life in the Church worked. As an eligible returned missionary, Matt found it difficult to date girls casually without hurting their feelings. Dating outside the Church was just as bad because it brought constant advice from his member friends.

Two Sundays before, he had searched for Shaye at church, hoping to pass her in the halls. He had even tried to come up with some excuse to drop by her apartment before he left on a road trip with his team. Unfortunately, he had not even seen Brooke or Jill since the swimming party. Stopping by the swimming pool on campus had not been a successful venture either, as he quickly concluded that she was not a member of the college's team.

Matt hit the ball one last time and stepped out of the batter's box, clearing the way for the next person in line.

A few hours later, as the bleachers began to fill for their first home game of spring training, Matt found himself thinking more about the singles activity that would be held the following day than about his first professional game. Would he finally get to talk to her at the barbecue and fireside? Would she even be there?

Nerves gnawed at his stomach as he took his position at first base. The stands were not even half full when the first pitch was thrown. As the pitcher tried to settle into his groove, Matt loosened up, and the plays began to fall into place.

During his team's first at-bat, he watched his first two teammates fail to claim a base. When he strode to the plate, anxiety had his stomach churning. The first pitch blew by him in the strike zone, and the second crowded him inside. By the third pitch, Matt shifted his weight back and powered his bat against the ball. Before he reached second base, the ball sailed over the left field fence.

The mascot, a grizzly bear, jumped up and down, trying to get the crowd involved. Even Matt had to admit that the bear looked more like a teddy bear than a fierce grizzly.

As the game progressed, Matt again found himself in a starring role. Throughout college, his name had been plastered all over the newspapers for his hitting ability. Occasionally, he was even recognized for his fielding skills and his speed.

A single on his second trip to the plate earned him an RBI, and only a walk in the eighth inning disrupted his perfect batting average. As he left the field after their first home win, Matt waved off the two reporters attempting to interview him.

As he settled in front of his television at home that night, Matt congratulated himself for staying out of the papers. He doubted that minor-league ball players made interesting copy anyway, but he figured he didn't want to take any chances now that Shaye was in close proximity. He could only stare when he saw himself on the highlights of the evening news.

CHAPTER 5

Music was blaring from behind the modest house when Matt arrived. The barbecue was being held in the backyard and would be followed by a singles fireside. He climbed out of his car, wincing from the strained muscle in his shoulder. His game had ended only an hour before, and he was beginning to wonder how professional ball players kept up with the pace. They had spent several hours two nights before on a plane flying in from Florida, where they had finished up a nine-day road trip.

He glanced around, surprised at the number of cars already parked along the street. They were still a couple of days away from March, yet the backyard barbecue appeared to have drawn a crowd. Of course, unlike Virginians, Texans expected to have temperatures hovering around sixty degrees this time of year.

As he approached the house, several other members of his ward arrived, and soon they found themselves in the expansive backyard. Their bishop was working the grill, and their host, Brother Foster, was overseeing the volleyball game already in progress. Caitlin and Leslie walked in just minutes later, and Leslie made a beeline for Matt. Instinctively, Matt stepped away from Leslie before she could make physical contact, leaving Caitlin standing between them.

"I saw you on the news last night." Leslie's lips formed a pout. "Why didn't you tell me you were a professional baseball player?"

"I'm just a minor leaguer." Matt shrugged, surprised to find out she had paid any attention to the news.

"Still, it has to be fascinating," Leslie gushed.

"Do you like baseball?" he asked, not really expecting an honest answer.

"Oh, I love baseball!"

Matt just nodded.

"How do you like your new team?" Caitlin asked.

"It's different," Matt admitted as more of their friends joined them.

As Leslie found a new audience, Matt turned to Caitlin. "Who all is coming to this activity? I don't recognize many people here."

"Just the young single adults in our stake. Don't worry. I'll introduce you around tonight."

"I may take you up on that." Matt scanned the crowd, searching.

"You know, we may have to come see you play sometime," Caitlin told him.

"Actually, I can probably get some free tickets if you want. I get a few for each game," Matt offered.

"You had better not say that too loud." Caitlin's gaze shifted to Leslie.

"We'll just keep it our secret . . ." Matt's voice trailed off, and he turned toward the house. Even from across the yard, he heard her voice and sensed her presence.

She stepped onto the patio and greeted those near the door, making her way toward Brooke. When Shaye turned toward him, their eyes met, and a smile came to her lips before she could stop it. She hesitated a moment before turning away and joining her roommate.

Caitlin put her hand on Matt's arm, breaking him out of his trance. "Come on. I'll introduce you."

"What?" Matt looked down at her, dazed.

Caitlin just laughed and pulled on his sleeve. "I promised to introduce you around. We're starting with Kylie."

"Kylie?" Matt fell into step with Caitlin as they made their way across the crowded yard.

"Kylie Ramsey," Caitlin elaborated.

Brooke greeted them as they approached. "Hi, Cait. Hi, Matt."

Kylie turned and found herself staring into Matt's blue eyes. Fighting instinct, she forced herself to stay where she was.

"I see you already know each other." Caitlin smiled at Brooke. "Kylie, have you met Matt Whitmore? He's new in our ward."

Matt offered his hand, his eyes sparkling mischievously as Kylie took it. "Nice to meet you." Matt smiled. "I saw you swimming the other day. I was impressed."

"Thanks," Kylie managed. She had prepared herself for his touch, yet it did nothing to diminish the impact. Warmth spread through her as he clasped her hand, running his thumb over her fingers. She noticed the fresh calluses on his palms and found herself staring into his eyes. Questions raced through her mind. What was he doing here? Had Doug arranged for him to be here, and if so, why hadn't Doug said anything?

"She never believes us when we tell her she's awesome," Brooke teased.

"They tend to exaggerate." Kylie realized her hand was still in Matt's and forced herself to pull it away.

"I doubt that." Matt shifted his weight from one foot to the other.

Kylie glanced over at their hostess standing in the doorway. "I had better go help Sister Foster." Though she forced herself to look at Matt as she stepped back, her expression was carefully guarded. "It was nice meeting you, Matt."

Matt nodded, his eyes following her as she retreated into the house.

"Typical," Brooke muttered.

"What?" Matt raised an eyebrow.

"Every time a guy comes near her, she goes running," Brooke told him.

Matt held back a grin. "She doesn't date much?"

"She doesn't date ever," Brooke told him. "Says she has bad luck when it comes to men."

"I know the feeling," Matt muttered, wondering what to do now that he knew her name.

As everyone fixed their plates at the large buffet table, Matt's eyes searched for Kylie. He was starting to think that she had left when he saw her come out of the house with a plate of food. She sat down under a tree on the far side of the yard next to Brooke.

Matt didn't realize he was holding up the food line until Caitlin nudged him along. "Why don't you just go sit with her?"

"What?" Matt grabbed his eating utensils and moved away from the table.

Caitlin stepped next to him and nodded toward Kylie. "Matt, I'd have to be blind not to notice how you look at her. Maybe you can change her luck with men."

"I don't know . . ."

"Besides, Leslie's got her eye on you," Caitlin warned.

Matt looked behind them and saw Leslie moving toward them. "I guess it's worth a try."

He walked across the yard, his shadow falling across Kylie and Brooke in the evening sun. "Do you mind if I join you?"

Brooke looked up and then over at Kylie. "Have a seat."

"Thanks." Matt sat down next to Kylie, ignoring the look of discomfort in her eyes.

"You know, I forgot to get something to drink." Brooke stood up as her green eyes flashed with mischief.

"Do you want me to get it for you?" Matt offered, moving to stand.

Brooke waved him off. "No, no. I'm fine." Matt didn't miss the wink she gave Kylie before moving off in the direction of the buffet table.

"Have you lived in Texas long?" Matt asked innocently as a couple passed by.

"About a year." Kylie took a sip from her water bottle, fiddling with the cap before she set it down beside her.

"Really?" Matt glanced around, grateful that they were somewhat secluded from everyone else. "It was just over a year ago that my girl-friend was killed."

Their eyes met briefly before Kylie looked down at the ground. She pulled her jacket tighter around her against the February breeze.

Memories washed over him at the simple gesture—the first time she had worn his letter jacket, the day they had gone shopping for her first real winter coat, the day she had seen snow falling for the first time. The warmth of the memories were quickly followed by the recollection of the day he had spent searching for her, finally finding her at the subway station right before he had been shot by the man sent to assassinate her. He took a deep breath, staring out into the middle distance of the yard. "This has been a hard year. I loved her very much."

Kylie glanced around, apparently making sure that no one else was within earshot. Still, she lowered her voice. "How did you find me?"

"I didn't." Matt's eyes met hers. "I moved here about a month ago. I had no idea you were here too until I saw you swimming."

"Matt, I'm serious. Did Doug tell you where I was?"

Matt shook his head, a smile playing on his lips.

Kylie's eyes widened. "You just happened to move into the same stake as me?"

Matt nodded. "I haven't heard from Doug in months. Besides, you know he would never tell me where you were. He worries too much about me being near you."

Kylie looked down at her hands, then back up at Matt. "I don't think this is a good idea."

"What?"

"You. Me. Together." Reluctantly, she turned away.

Matt studied her for a moment. He recognized the doubts and knew her well enough to know that much of her concern was for his safety, even more than for her own. Logically, he knew there was some risk if they were together, but after spending the last year without the benefit of her presence in his life, even in the form of phone calls, he found himself pushing aside his concerns. After all, they were in the same town, whether they talked to each other or not. Why not enjoy their friendship once again? "You know, a friend of mine told me not long ago I should start dating again. I think it's about time I started taking his advice."

"Somehow, I don't think I'm what your friend had in mind." Kylie tried to keep her voice cool, but her lips quirked up at his reference to Doug.

Matt leaned back on one elbow, ignoring the food in front of him. "I made a mistake once of not telling someone I cared about who I am and who my father is. But that was in Virginia. My family is more than a thousand miles away."

Kylie looked at him, knowing that it was the associations of his family members that had put her life in danger before. Matt by himself would not have jeopardized her cover. She took a deep breath, a glimmer of hope spreading through her. "What brought you to Texas?"

"Baseball."

"You dropped out of college to play baseball?" Surprise laced her voice. "I thought you turned down the chance to play professionally."

Matt shook his head. "I graduated early, and I got another offer to play in the minor leagues." He leaned closer, his voice almost a whisper. "Besides, I didn't have a reason to stay in Virginia anymore."

Kylie's heartbeat quickened as a smile spread across her face. She shook her head in disbelief.

"So, do you want to go out to dinner sometime?" Matt disarmed her with his smile.

"I dated a guy once that never took no for an answer." Kylie kept her eyes focused on his. "You remind me of him. A lot."

"How about tomorrow night?" Matt asked. Before she could answer, he added, "I'll pick you up around seven."

"On one condition." Kylie looked out over the yard, already noticing some speculative glances being cast their way. "We keep this between us. I don't want us to turn into the couple of the month."

"Does that mean I have to hang out with Leslie?" Matt cringed.

Kylie stifled a giggle. "You know, she's planning on asking you out."

"Are you enjoying this?" Matt picked at his food. "Shouldn't you at least get jealous or something?"

"I did."

Amusement flickered briefly in Matt's eyes. "Are you at least going to let me pick you up at your apartment?"

Kylie nodded. "Let's just take it slow."

* * *

"I can't believe it." Brooke dropped down on the couch and put her feet up on the coffee table. "You had a shot at the stake's most eligible bachelor, and nothing."

Jill joined her on the couch, cradling a cup of hot chocolate. She glanced briefly at the stack of tests she still needed to grade, but then focused back on the subject at hand. "I thought for sure he would sit with you during the fireside."

Kylie glanced up from the textbook she was reading and rereading, looking adequately bored.

"And how could you chase him away and leave him defenseless against Leslie, of all people?" Brooke threw her arms up in dismay.

"What's wrong with Leslie?" Kylie asked innocently.

"For one thing, Matt isn't interested in her at all, and she was practically throwing herself at the poor guy," Jill told her.

"How do you know he's not interested in her?" Kylie raised an eyebrow, wondering how observant her roommates had been.

"She was hitting on him at the swimming party a few weeks ago, and he couldn't get away from her fast enough." Jill sipped her hot chocolate.

"Maybe he changed his mind." Kylie shrugged.

"Oh, please!" Brooke looked from Kylie to Jill. "Will you talk some sense into her?"

"Don't look at me. At least you got them alone for a few minutes," Jill pointed out.

"For all the good that it did," Brooke muttered.

"At least tell us what happened when you talked to Matt." Jill pulled Kylie's textbook out of her hands.

"Jill!" Kylie reached for her book unsuccessfully.

"Tell." Jill hugged the book to her chest.

"There's nothing to tell," Kylie insisted. "He said he's still hung up on an old girlfriend, he's from Virginia, and he's new in town."

"He was talking about an old girlfriend?" Brooke raised her eyebrows. "That's interesting."

"Brooke, get off it." Kylie stood and snatched her book from Jill. "I'm going to study."

Jill waited until Kylie's door closed. "She really likes him."

"Oh yeah," Brooke agreed.

CHAPTER 6

Doug Valdez stared at the file on his desk, willing it to share some new insight with him. For more than a year he had studied, analyzed, and dissected this case. Yet still he knew it wasn't over. He turned and looked at the photos tacked to the wall of his cubicle. Most were mug shots, taken at the time of arrest of the many men who had worked in Chris Rush's organization. They were arranged neatly in an organizational chart, with Chris Rush's photo at the top, and the lowest of his thugs on the bottom tier. But there were holes, and Doug knew it.

Half a dozen other agents worked alongside him in similar cubicles, but it was rare for Doug to consult with them on this case. He was vaguely aware of the phones ringing, the constant clicking of keyboards in use, and the odor of stale coffee that hung in the air. If he stood up, he would be able to see the Dallas skyline against the crisp blue sky through the window across the office. Rarely did he take the time to notice the view or anything else happening around him while he was working.

He had been assigned to Dallas three years before after spending his first several years with the Bureau in Washington, D.C. In fact, he had been called in to set up surveillance during Kylie's first relocation when threats arose. When her previous agent-in-charge had been shot in the line of duty, Doug had taken over her case. Relocating her just a two-hour drive from Dallas had been a convenience for him and unexpected enough that no one would go looking for her so near without a tip-off.

He also had the added benefit of having his sister nearby, so he often used the excuse of going to see her when he needed to check in on Kylie. He glanced down at the latest photograph of his nephews that sat on the corner of his desk. The older sported a new gap in his smile, and the younger one was already looking more like a little boy than a toddler.

The wave of envy surprised him, as did the desire to have a family of his own. His sister was barely two years his elder, yet at thirty she had already been married for eight years and was expecting her third child in just a few months. He thought of the woman he was supposed to go out with that evening, all too aware that she wasn't the sort he would ever take home to meet the folks. His mother would undoubtedly disapprove of the short skirts and low-cut tops she often wore. His father would certainly share that opinion. He also doubted that his parents would have much interest in his date's single-minded obsession with working out.

With a shake of his head, Doug flipped to the next page in the file and studied the photo of one of Rush's middlemen. Just thirteen months before, the man had attempted to recruit a U.S. Marshal to feed information back to him. Specifically, he wanted the new name and location of Christal Jones, a.k.a. Shaye Kendall.

The marshal had enough sense to lead the guy along and then to gather enough evidence to incriminate him for attempted bribery. Still, Doug and his superiors knew that while that attempt had failed, it was unlikely that Rush and his colleagues would give up. Kylie's information would continue to be classified at the highest level, on a strictly need-to-know basis, especially until Doug could determine if Rush's underlings had succeeded in recruiting a government official to give them the details they so desperately wanted.

Doug knew the FBI and U.S. Marshals were using Kylie as bait. Otherwise, the FBI would have long ago handed her case over to the marshals for her protection and moved on to the next operation. He hadn't really cared at first. After all, Kylie Ramsey was the means to the end of one of the largest smuggling operations in recent history. Drugs, weapons, jewels, people. The organization's only consistent criteria as to what they would smuggle was simply that it be profitable.

Over the past year, however, he had somehow become more personally involved in the case. He could remember all too clearly the first time he read her file. He had actually laughed out loud when he learned that some innocent little Mormon girl needed protection. As he had skimmed over her data, however, he had been amazed that she had survived the day her boyfriend was murdered.

More than one person on the Rush case had referred to it as a miracle. Doug had always brushed it off as luck until she miraculously escaped from Rush's men again almost entirely on her own. Sometimes he wondered how many more miracles she had saved up.

Yet every time Kylie was called on to testify, he was all too aware that she became a target again. During the early months after Chris Rush's arrest, many of the men in the organization had plea-bargained for lighter sentences. Recently, however, an increasing number of Rush's men were insisting their cases go all the way to trial. Doug was convinced that they were trying to force Kylie to testify so that they could once again attempt to kill her.

"Coffee?" Liz Fielder, the newest member of the Dallas office, held out a styrofoam cup, steam rising from the dark liquid inside.

"No thanks." Doug leaned back in his chair, glancing up at Liz. She was older than him by a dozen years, but she went to great lengths to maintain her youthful appearance. Her face was carefully made up, and gray hair was simply not permitted in the glossy chestnut mane that fell to her shoulders. She wore a navy blazer over matching slacks and a simple white blouse, simple yet dignified.

"Still working on the Jones case?"

Doug nodded, closing the file he had been studying. "Can't be too careful these days."

"Let me know if you need any help." With the coffee still in hand, Liz wandered to the next cubicle.

Doug flipped open another file, this one outlining Kylie's last court appearance. Unbeknownst to Kylie, a murder attempt had been thwarted at her hotel just hours before she testified. They were still unable to determine if her hotel information had been leaked by someone inside the FBI or if a member of the hotel staff had somehow given out the information.

As he began to prepare for the next court appearance, Doug knew he had to be ready for anything.

* * *

Kylie breathed a sigh of relief when the door closed behind Jill and Brooke as they left with their dates. She had not realized that they had plans until after she had made plans of her own. Throughout the day she had rehearsed in her mind what she would say to her roommates when Matt arrived to pick her up. Now that she was alone, she knew she wasn't quite ready for the speculation about her and Matt, even from her roommates.

Since accepting Matt's invitation to dinner, she had been preparing herself for the reality of dating again, especially now that she had friends to share her feelings with. Of course, she would have to censor those feelings about Matt when she talked with her roommates. Though she trusted them completely, she couldn't let anyone know that Matt had been part of a former life.

The bad dreams had increased since seeing him at the swimming party. Often she awoke with vague impressions of the past on the edge of her consciousness. Each time, her heart pounded with terror and dread. She knew she was being selfish by letting him back into her life, but her need to be with him had overwhelmed her the moment she first saw him again.

It had been a fluke that the man responsible for her old boyfriend's murder just happened to be a friend and associate of Matt's father. Like so many others in the Washington, D.C., area, Senator Whitmore had believed Chris Rush to be an honorable man. After more than a year, it was unlikely that anyone would even suspect Matt of making contact with her, especially since the general public believed that her would-be murderer had succeeded.

Kylie's heart went into overdrive when the doorbell rang. She had imagined letting him in, being taken into his arms, and feeling the warmth of his embrace. She tried to shove disappointment aside when Matt didn't even come into her apartment, instead waiting for her to join him outside.

The way he walked beside her, avoiding physical contact, reminded her of their first dates when they had started their relationship as friends. He opened the car door for her, and Kylie climbed in, remembering too vividly the last time she had occupied this seat. She had been running for her life then, and Matt had been the person she had turned to for help.

The silence between them was awkward as Matt drove to the restaurant. Finally, after they were settled at their table, Kylie initiated conversation.

"Why don't you tell me about yourself," she suggested, laying her menu aside.

"Not much to tell. My brother Charlie is on a mission in Canada, and my sister Amy will graduate from high school this spring." Matt hesitated, and the loneliness they had shared apart during the past year was all too visible in his eyes. "What about you?"

Kylie's eyebrows shot up. She knew he was really asking what her cover story was now. "I moved here from Florida just over a year ago. The bishop here helped find me an apartment. That's how I met Brooke and Jill."

"And you swim," Matt prodded.

"I swim with a private coach along with a few other people who are planning to compete in the Olympic trials next year." Kylie shrugged her shoulders. Remembering whom she was with, she added, "And hopefully the Olympics."

"Why don't you swim on the college team?" His blue eyes stared intently as though they were the only two people in the room.

"Have you seen them?" Shaye asked.

Matt laughed. "Yeah, I have. I guess that would be taking a step backward for you."

"I know that sounds conceited, but it would," Kylie admitted.

"You don't seem like the type who is too full of herself," Matt assured her as the waiter arrived to take their order.

Over dinner, they caught up on the past year. They talked about many things, both of them avoiding any mention of Doug. The uncomfortable silences that had plagued them earlier were replaced with conversation fitting of best friends. And though the words were not said, their eyes expressed the loneliness they had each felt during their separation.

As they left the restaurant, an awkward distance settled between them. After spending so many nights dreaming of the kisses they had shared and, more importantly, the friendship that had grown between them, Kylie couldn't understand why Matt now took such care not to touch her in even the most casual way. When Matt stood outside her apartment to drop her off, he said good night without so much as a handshake.

"Matt, what's going on here?"

Matt turned back to face her. "What do you mean?"

"Are you afraid to touch me?" Kylie crossed her arms, hurt and loneliness flickering in her eyes.

He stepped toward her, caressing her cheek with his hand. "This is only our first date. It wouldn't be appropriate . . ."

"I see." Kylie paused a moment, and then her stance relaxed. She smiled and stepped toward the door. "Wait here for a minute."

Matt opened his mouth, but before he could say anything, he was standing on her doorstep alone. A moment later, she reappeared after discarding her jacket and pulling on a sweatshirt.

"I'm ready for our second date now." Mischief flashed in her slate-gray eyes.

His laughter escaped him as he took her arm. "I like the way you think. Shall we go get some dessert?"

"There's an ice cream parlor a couple of blocks away." Kylie grinned.

As they stood out in the cool night air eating ice cream, Matt leaned on his car next to Kylie. "Weren't you the one who suggested we take things slow?"

"I guess I was," Kylie admitted. She popped the last bite of her ice cream cone into her mouth.

"You know, I've never had two dates in one night before." Matt wiped his hand on a napkin and then tossed it into a nearby trash can.

"Really?" Kylie reached for his hand, needing the physical contact with him.

Matt laced his fingers with hers and stepped closer. "Would it be too forward of me to kiss you right now?"

"Technically, this is our second date," Kylie reminded him with a smile.

With his free hand, Matt caressed her cheek, leaning down to brush his lips against hers. Memories came flooding back of their last moments together as he reveled in the softness of her skin and the warmth of her kiss. And when they separated, her eyes were clouded with emotions, but this time there was joy, not fear.

"I've missed you," Kylie said softly as she let Matt pull her into an embrace. She closed her eyes, breathing in the scent of him.

"I love you," Matt whispered in her ear, surprised that the words still came so easily.

Kylie pulled back so she could see his eyes. "I love you too."

* * *

The apartment was empty when Kylie walked in after her dates with Matt. After realizing that Jill and Brooke were still out, Kylie was disappointed to find herself alone. Even though she had been grateful to begin her first date without her roommates' knowledge, she ached to talk to someone about the man who had come back into her life.

Brooke and Jill had become her family over the past year. She imagined them being the older sisters she never had, though Brooke was only older than her by a few months. Without her friends to turn to, Kylie turned to the one person who had been with her through all three of her identities.

Inside her room, Kylie knelt by her bed and poured out her heart to her Heavenly Father. Just expressing her gratitude and acknowledging that He had brought Matt back into her life filled her with the Spirit. She shared her doubts and concerns and even dared to express her hopes for the future.

When she rose, she picked up the stuffed dolphin on her bed. She had taken it from Chase's apartment the night he was killed, just a month after her father had died of a heart attack. Chase had been her first love, and time had still not completely healed her heart.

Falling for Matt and losing him less than a year after the deaths of Chase and her father had been devastating. Only the safety and security she had found here in Texas had helped her heart to mend. Now with Matt back in her life, she hoped she could finally gamble on love and win.

When she heard the front door closing followed by voices, she settled the little dolphin back on her bed. As she joined Brooke and Jill in the living room, she knew she could keep her secret a little longer.

* * *

Matt padded across the cool ceramic tile into the kitchen. He couldn't sleep. His mind was still racing as he replayed the night's events in his mind.

How many times had he dreamed of finding her again? Of holding her again? And now she was really here. The nervousness that had been part of her when they had first met had been replaced by serenity. He sensed that she felt safe here, and he was determined to keep it that way.

He had put her in danger before, and he vowed he would do everything he could to keep her out of harm's way now that he was part of her life again. But even though he could easily imagine kneeling across the altar from her, he knew they still had a huge obstacle between them: Chris Rush.

The last time Matt had spoken with his father, the trial date had been pushed back yet again and was currently set for May. Unless it was moved again, they would be free of that obstacle in just three more months.

Matt pulled a carton of Chinese food out of the refrigerator and dumped it into a bowl. He took a bite of the cold beef and broccoli before reconsidering and warming it in the microwave. With food in hand, he sat on the floor in his bedroom and pulled a suitcase out of the closet. Laying it on the floor, he opened it reverently.

He fingered the worn Bible nestled in the clothes. The sweatshirts and shorts were packed neatly. Several swimming suits were rolled into balls, and a stack of swim caps was tucked under two new pairs of goggles.

Matt had gone through the suitcase more than a year before. He wondered if the FBI even knew that he had it. After the reports of Shaye's death, her roommate, Colleen, had brought Shaye's belongings to Matt, knowing that she had no family.

Matt knew that her clothing and swimming apparatus had been replaced long ago, but he had the one thing she had lost that had been irreplaceable. He pulled the manila envelope from the inside pocket of the suitcase. Dumping the contents on the floor, he stared down at the man in the photo with Kylie.

She had never shown him the picture before, but Matt knew who it was. Chase. Her dead boyfriend.

Matt knew he shouldn't feel threatened by him, but one concern had plagued him since finding it in her luggage so long ago. Did she love him as much as she had loved Chase? And if Chase hadn't died, would she have even been part of his life?

She looked so happy in the photo with one arm wrapped around Chase and the other holding her father close. Had he ever seen her look so carefree before? Matt had to admit that the girl in the photo was a stranger to him. He knew that she had lost her mother at an early age and had little or no memory of her. Yet when he studied her expression in the photo, Kylie appeared to be happy, safe, and looking forward to the possibilities life had to offer. Those possibilities had disappeared so quickly after the two men in the photo died only a month apart.

With one last look, Matt slipped the photo back into the envelope and repacked the suitcase. As he shuffled the items in his closet, a framed sketch fell onto the floor. He caught his breath at his own creation.

He had not even known her when he had drawn it, but something about her had intrigued him even then. Her identity was hidden by her hooded sweatshirt, which was why he could keep it now. The other sketches he had drawn of her had been locked away by the FBI until after the trial.

Rummaging through the bottom of his closet, he finally found a hammer and a nail. He walked into the living room and hammered the nail into the wall. Then, as though staking his claim, he hung the portrait so that it would be the first thing he would see every time he walked through his front door.

CHAPTER 7

Matt stood in the middle of his apartment, making one last inspection. Just the week before, he had purchased a large throw rug to warm the room. The deep blue and cream in the rug matched the throw pillows on his couch. An end table sat between the couch and matching chair, with an *Ensign* magazine sitting next to the lamp.

He had to admit that the apartment could have belonged to anybody. Only the single framed sketch gave the room any character. Everything else that expressed his personality was tucked away in his bedroom. His drawing table occupied the corner of his room, with his baseball equipment hidden in his closet. A few sketches of his favorite baseball players adorned the walls. Cal Ripken, Jr., had won the prized spot facing the bedroom door.

Matt wasn't sure how he had gotten roped into hosting family home evening at his apartment, but someone had deemed it his turn. His feelings had been mixed when he had attended family home evening two weeks before. Though he felt comfortable with most of the other young single adults in their ward, keeping Leslie at arm's length was a challenge. For that reason alone, he looked forward to the day that Leslie would realize he was dating someone else. Of course, with his baseball schedule, his attendance at family home evenings would be sporadic at best, since he would continue to be out of town half the time throughout the season.

When he opened the door for his guests, he wasn't surprised when Leslie came sauntering through first. Veronica and Caitlin followed, each holding a plate.

"We brought refreshments with us," Caitlin told him.

Veronica led the way to the kitchen. "We guessed that you're still playing the starving bachelor."

"Something like that," Matt admitted. He had thrown away all of the pizza boxes before they arrived.

"Have you gotten all settled in?" Leslie asked, surveying the room.

"I'm getting there." Matt opened the refrigerator and took out a soda. "Help yourself to something to drink."

Leslie's eyes landed on the sketch, and she crossed the room to take a closer look.

"Thanks." Caitlin pulled out a soda for herself and snatched a cookie off the plate Veronica had just unwrapped.

Matt followed suit, not even wincing when Veronica slapped at his hand. He just winked at her as he popped the cookie into his mouth.

Leslie stepped closer to them, pouting. "I didn't realize you and Kylie were an item."

"Excuse me?" Matt choked.

"It looks just like her." Leslie shifted her gaze back to the sketch on the wall.

Matt shook his head. "I drew that during college of my old girl-friend."

"Really?" Hope dawned in Leslie's eyes again.

Veronica crossed the room to study the drawing. "It does seem to resemble Kylie Ramsey a bit." She turned to look at Matt. "Have you met her yet?"

Caitlin answered for him. "I introduced them at the cookout."

"Where is your old girlfriend now?" Leslie asked, nodding toward the sketch.

Matt shifted his weight. His voice was low when he formed the words. "She was killed last year."

"Oh, Matt. That's terrible." Caitlin reached out, laying her hand on his arm.

Matt just shrugged, grateful for the distraction of the doorbell. Shortly after the other members of their family home evening group arrived, everyone settled down in the living room.

After Caitlin gave the lesson she had prepared, the socializing began. Everyone was just digging into the refreshments when Matt's profession became the topic of conversation.

"We were all talking about coming to a game this week," Veronica told him. She grinned mischievously as she added, "That is, if you guys are any good."

"You'll just have to come and see," Matt replied. "What game did you want to come to?"

"Probably the one on Friday," Caitlin stated.

"Hold on a second." Matt strode across the room and opened his bedroom door. He picked up an envelope off of his dresser and slid six of the ten tickets out of it. He turned to go to the living room again, but was surprised that Leslie was blocking the doorway.

She surveyed the room, her gaze settling on the drafting table. "Do you still draw much?"

Matt shook his head. "Not since college."

"Maybe I could model for you sometime," Leslie suggested, leaning on the doorjamb.

"Sorry. I gave up portraits a long time ago."

She stepped back just far enough for Matt to squeeze through as he approached the door.

Ignoring Leslie, Matt pulled the door closed behind him. "Here, Caitlin. There's no reason for you to pay for tickets."

"Thanks, Matt."

"Are there enough for all of us?" Leslie asked, her pout ready.

"Yes, Leslie," Caitlin said patiently. She turned to the other guys in their group. "Did you guys want to come too?"

Garth, the most soft-spoken of the men, came to life. "Yeah, that would be great!"

As everyone started organizing rides, Matt's phone rang. He stepped into the kitchen to answer it.

"Hello." Matt struggled to focus in spite of the laughter in his living room.

"Matt, I'm glad I caught you at home." Jim Whitmore's voice came over the phone.

"What's up, Dad?" Matt tensed at the tone of his father's voice.

"I just got a call from the FBI. Chris Rush's trial has been delayed again." Disappointment filled Jim's voice. "I thought you would want to know."

Matt tried to keep a leash on his temper. "Isn't this ever going to end?"

"We just have to be patient." Jim's voice soothed. "I know this is hard on you."

Realizing his guests were watching him, Matt lowered his voice. "Look, I'll have to call you back."

"Okay, but as it stands now, the trial will be in August."

"Thanks for letting me know." Matt hung up, overwhelmed with frustration.

Leslie appeared at his side before he had gotten his emotions under control. With a hand on his arm, she asked, "Is everything okay?"

"Yeah." Matt pulled away from her.

"If there's anything I can do . . ." Leslie batted her eyelashes and pushed her hair behind her shoulder.

Matt just shook his head, grateful that Veronica and Caitlin insisted that it was getting late. A few minutes later, Matt found himself alone in his apartment.

Within five minutes, he was lacing up his shoes as he prepared to relieve his frustrations. He stepped into the cool night air and started running without a destination in mind. When he found himself at the college, he made his way to the swimming pool.

He stepped into the building and spotted her immediately. Judging from her determination, he guessed she had just received a similar phone call. After stretching for a few minutes, Matt settled down on a bench and watched her.

She was swimming the breaststroke, which typically meant she was deep in thought. Matt watched her, surprised. When he had known her previously, she had been forbidden to swim the breast-stroke for fear that someone in the swimming community might recognize her. He breathed a sigh of relief when twenty minutes later, she switched to freestyle. He assumed correctly that she was starting her cooldown.

When she climbed out of the pool, she almost ran right into him. "Matt . . ." Her breathing had not yet returned to normal. "What are you doing here?"

"I went for a run and ended up here." He stared down at her. "I got a disturbing phone call tonight from my dad."

Kylie shook her head and looked down at the pool. "It's not fair."

"I know." Matt pulled her into his arms, ignoring the water still dripping from her.

The tears came even though she tried to fight them. And while Matt held her, they both knew that their future wasn't really theirs until after the trial of Chris Rush.

When she stepped away from Matt, she was torn between her tears and laughter. Matt's clothes were soaked. "I'm sorry, Matt."

Matt glanced down at his wet shirt and shrugged. "It'll dry." He nodded toward the locker room. "Go ahead and change. I'll wait for you."

When Kylie reappeared a few minutes later, Matt fell into step with her just as he had done so many times before. He slipped his arm around her shoulder, not even noticing her slight hesitation as they walked outside to her car.

"Do you want a ride home?" Kylie asked as she disengaged her car alarm and unlocked the door.

Matt nodded. "Sure."

Kylie followed Matt's directions to his apartment and parked next to his car.

"Can I talk you into coming in for a while?" Matt's eyes pleaded with her. "I could use a friend to talk to right now."

After a quick glance around the parking lot, Kylie nodded. She got out of the car and followed him to his apartment. She thought it ironic that when they had dated before, he had so many friends that they were always running into someone he knew. At the time, she had yet to develop any close friendships. Now she had two wonderful friends she could share almost anything with, and Matt was the new guy in town.

Kylie gasped when he turned on the light. She had only seen that portrait of herself once before, and its effect was still just as powerful. Even though the mystery that shrouded the girl in the sketch was buried deep within her now, Matt had captured the intrigue beautifully the night he had first seen her.

"When this is all behind us, I want to display the whole series of sketches in our house," Matt told her.

Kylie blinked hard, looking from the sketch to Matt. He had professed his love before, but he had never mentioned marriage.

Matt took her hand and led her to the couch. He sat by her, rubbing his thumb absently over her hand. "Tell me what you've heard."

"Doug called tonight." Kylie leaned her head back and stared at the ceiling. "He said the trial has been moved back again."

"My dad said it's set for August now."

Kylie felt tears threaten, and she blinked them back. "Doug thinks Rush is trying to postpone it as long as possible, hoping they can find me at the Olympic trials."

"Next year?" Matt asked incredulously.

Kylie nodded, annoyed at the single tear that spilled over. "The FBI will never let me compete until after I testify against him."

"I thought they were hoping he believed the story that you were killed."

"All that story did was buy them some time." Kylie's eyes met his, suddenly aware of the weight lifting from her shoulders as Matt shared her burden. "I've already testified in seventeen trials so far."

"What?" Matt tensed.

"Seventeen," Kylie repeated. "The first two were for Chase's killers right before I was relocated here. The rest have been related to the drug cartel and smuggling operation that Rush masterminded."

Matt thought of the picture in his closet. He started to go get it for her, but he pushed the idea aside with just a twinge of guilt. "Then Rush knows you're alive and well."

"Probably." Kylie nodded. "Everyone at the FBI is optimistic that once he's behind bars for good, I'll be able to come out of protective custody. They've already convicted most of the middlemen in Rush's organization, and more than a hundred have plea-bargained for lighter sentences."

"Aren't they worried about retribution?" Matt asked, concerned.

"They've talked about tightening security if I do make the Olympic team, but if they convict Rush, he'll be behind bars for good." Kylie squeezed his hand, ignoring the fear that crept up her spine every time she thought of Chris Rush and what he was capable of. "Honestly, he deserves it."

"You won't get any argument out of me," Matt agreed. "When I was watching you tonight, you were swimming the breaststroke. I didn't think you were supposed to swim it anymore because your stroke might be recognized."

"It's risky for me to swim at all, but there's no way I can get ready for the Olympics if I wait to start training until after Rush's trial." Kylie shrugged. "Doug kept me out of competitive swimming for over a month when I first moved here. Then he found a private coach with a small, year-round team. Ryan, my coach, only works with swimmers who can make national cuts."

"But I thought you couldn't swim nationals." Matt looked at her, confused.

"I came here too late to swim in nationals last year. I wasn't in good enough shape, so I've only competed in some of the smaller regional meets." A sigh escaped her as she leaned closer to Matt. "Now it looks like Doug will be inventing some kind of injury or family emergency when nationals come up this year."

"I'm sorry." Matt turned, finding his face close to Kylie's. The vulnerability was there again, just beneath the surface, as it had been when he first met her. His heart ached for the young woman she had been, abruptly displaced from the future she had planned for herself before witnessing Chase's murder. Gently he pressed his lips to hers, his fingers tangling in the thickness of her damp hair. The sensation was the same as it had been before, yet somehow different.

Kylie freed herself from his embrace and stood up. "I should go."

Though Matt wanted to stretch out their time together, he knew she was right. "I'll walk you out."

A car sped into the parking lot as they stepped outside. Kylie jumped back, startled. Her eyes widened, and fear paralyzed her as she watched the car speed toward them. The air exploded from her lungs when the car passed, screeching to a halt in front of the next apartment building.

As the teenage driver jumped out of the car and sauntered into the next building, Kylie willed her heartbeat to slow. She scolded herself for letting fear take over again, annoyed that the past could still reach into her present so easily.

"Are you okay?" Matt's arm tightened around her protectively. He recognized the fear in her eyes and found himself surprised to see that emotion in her now.

Kylie shrugged. "I try so hard not to be afraid, and then something so trivial can get me all worked up again."

"You can't just turn off your feelings."

"No, but I can keep fear from ruling my life." Kylie disengaged her car alarm. She turned and found herself encircled by Matt's strong arms. She leaned into his embrace, breathing him in. So many times over the past year she had wished for moments like this, having Matt to talk to, to confide in. Despite her friendship with her roommates, she couldn't count the number of times she wished she could just call Matt and tell him about her day, or have him simply reassure her that someone understood her difficult situation.

Matt held her for a moment longer, his hand linking with hers in a gesture of comfort. Finally, he stepped back and opened her car door. "When can I see you again?"

"I have midterms all week," Kylie told him regretfully. "How about Friday?"

"Great, if you want to come to a baseball game."

"I could do that." Kylie smiled at the thought of seeing him play. She had been relocated before baseball season when they were in college together.

"I'll drop the tickets by your apartment sometime this week," Matt told her. He leaned down and kissed her good-bye. "See you later."

"Bye." Kylie slid into her car, and with a last wave, she drove off into the night.

The faint smell of chlorine still lingered in his apartment as he settled down to watch the news. Somehow, just knowing that she had been here made this apartment seem a bit more like home.

CHAPTER 8

The room was small and airless, furnished only with a scarred table and a few chairs. Leonard Abbott set his briefcase down on the table and took a seat. Sweat beaded on his upper lip. Deliberately, he took his handkerchief from the inside pocket of his suit jacket and dabbed the perspiration away.

He hated this place. He hated the stench, the security, and mostly the reminder that he could end up here just as easily as his client had. Why else would the esteemed Judge Christopher Rush personally request him to be his lead council? The reason was simple. Blackmail.

Judge Rush had been on the bench when the district attorney had attempted to bring a case against him. Leonard had little recollection of exactly what happened the night in question, the night that a young man had been struck down and killed by a speeding car. His car.

In a moment of weakness, Leonard had pleaded with Judge Rush to help him. His desperation was so overwhelming that he hadn't thought twice about paying the sum of money the judge had requested. Only later would he realize that the money transfer could be documented on his side only. The judge had insisted he transfer the funds to a numbered account in the Cayman Islands, leaving the judge with the evidence against Leonard with little possibility of repercussion for his own actions.

Though the D.A. had felt the case was airtight, the judge had thrown it out on a technicality. The speculation about the sudden dismissal lasted for a few weeks, but ultimately Leonard Abbott was left to his boring practice in the Maryland suburbs with his wife and two kids. Now Leonard found himself even further indebted to his client, who had decided to collect again for that favor offered so long ago.

To maintain appearances, he opened his briefcase and retrieved a file. He agreed with Judge Rush that the case against him was largely superficial except for the damaging testimony Christal Jones could offer. He also knew that Rush had every intention of making sure she never made it to the courtroom. He tried not to think about that. The thought of witnesses disappearing made him queasy.

Still, since the only conversations that were guaranteed to remain private while Chris Rush was in custody were those with his lawyer, Leonard had been forced to play the important role of messenger within Rush's organization.

He rubbed his damp palms on his pants, turning abruptly when the door opened. The guard barely glanced at Leonard as he escorted Rush into the room. He was clothed in a bright orange prison uniform, but he didn't look any less formidable than he had sitting on the bench. His dark hair was now almost completely gray, his tan long gone since he could no longer visit the golf course with regularly. Despite these minor changes in appearance, he exuded an air of power. His eyes were dark and shrewd, but otherwise he looked like an attractive, middle-aged man who had the misfortune of ending up in a cell.

Rush took the seat opposite Leonard and looked up at the guard. He tapped his fingers impatiently as he waited for the guard to close the door and leave them alone. The moment the door closed, Rush reached across for the file in front of Leonard. He flipped it open and spoke without looking up. "Anything?"

"The continuance was approved. You have until August now." Leonard motioned to the file. "Your inside contact has fed information to your people several times, but the girl keeps getting away."

"Tell Malloy to increase the price." Rush looked up, his eyes hard. "I want this over."

* * *

Kylie was halfway through her sociology notes when the doorbell rang. Though she was eagerly waiting for Matt to drop by "sometime this week," she forced herself to stay seated.

Jill answered the door, and Kylie just smiled as her roommate's voice carried through the apartment.

"Matt, what a surprise." Jill stepped back. "Come on in."

Matt lifted a hand in greeting to Brooke and Kylie, who were both surrounded by textbooks. "I can't stay, but I thought you all might want tickets to the game Friday night."

"That was sweet of you to think of us." Jill took the tickets Matt offered her.

"You'll come too, won't you, Kylie?" Brooke insisted.

Kylie suppressed a smile. She tried to sound nonchalant as she said, "Sure, it sounds like fun."

"Are you expecting a home-cooked meal in return for these?" Jill asked, holding up the tickets.

"Just hoping," Matt laughed. "I'll see you later."

Kylie picked up her notes, wondering how she was supposed to concentrate now. Just as she figured out where she had left off, Brooke's voice broke through her thoughts.

"You will come Friday night, right?"

"I said I would." Kylie set her notebook in her lap. "Why are you making such a big deal about me going?"

"Because you're the reason Matt gave us those tickets," Brooke said knowingly.

Kylie just stared at her. She could hardly deny the truth, but she was clueless as to how Brooke had come to this conclusion.

Jill sat down on the floor next to the pile of homework she had been grading. "I think so too," she agreed. "I think he likes you."

"Just promise us that you'll at least give him a chance."

Kylie laughed out loud. She just couldn't keep it in.

"What?" Brooke threw her arms up in despair. "You haven't been out on a single date since you've lived here."

"Matt's just such a nice guy," Jill encouraged. "He deserves to find someone like you."

"Yeah," Brooke agreed. "Otherwise he might end up with someone like Leslie."

"Okay, so if Matt asks me out, I'll tell him I have my roommates' approval." Kylie tucked a lock of hair behind her ear. "Notice, I did say *if.*"

"I think it's more a matter of *when*," Brooke laughed.

* * *

"Do you see Matt?" Brooke asked anxiously as they made their way to their seats. The light breeze caught a strand of her dark auburn hair and teased it into her face. She brushed at it absently, pushing forward as though she knew exactly where they were going.

Jill was busy scanning the dugout, not noticing the appreciative glances being cast her way. "Not yet."

"Let's just find our seats." Kylie motioned to the section they were in, surprised that so many people were in the stands. Of course, the perfect spring weather was certainly motivation for a lot of people to get outside. As they got closer to the field, more and more of the seats were filled. Their own seats were just a few rows back, off to the side of the dugout.

"I should have brought my binoculars," Brooke muttered, following Jill to their section. She almost fell over when she looked up and saw Leslie sitting in the row behind them. Next to her were Veronica and Caitlin, and in the row behind them were three more people from Matt's ward.

Everyone exchanged greetings as they settled down in their seats. Leslie leaned forward on the back of Kylie's seat. "I guess you all came to see Matt play too."

Brooke nodded. "Is this the first game you've been to?"

"So far," Leslie answered. She eyed Kylie before asking, "How about you?"

"Us too," Jill told her.

Suddenly, Leslie jumped to her feet. "Oh, look! There he is!"

Kylie leaned back in her seat, embarrassed. She could just imagine how Matt would feel if he saw Leslie cheering for him for simply walking onto the field.

"Doesn't he look great in his uniform?" Leslie asked, rushing on before anyone could answer. "This is so exciting."

"Leslie, the game hasn't started yet," Brooke pointed out.

"Oh, Brooke. Don't be such a party pooper," Leslie scolded.

Kylie was grateful when the game actually started so that Leslie's narrative was drowned out by the rest of the crowd. She had to hold back her laughter when she heard Caitlin patiently explaining the rules of baseball to Leslie.

Leslie's high-pitched squeal annoyed everyone in their section when Matt stepped up to the plate for the first time. He hit a long ball over the fence in foul territory and ended up striking out. None of his teammates managed to get on base either during the first three innings.

The first score came from the other team when a ball dropped in front of the center fielder and a base runner scored. A second run was scored for the other team before the fourth inning ended.

The batter before Matt got a single. Kylie found herself holding her breath as Matt stepped up to the plate. The first pitch whizzed by him high and inside. On the second pitch, Matt knocked the ball over the fence again, this time in fair territory for a home run.

"I didn't know he was so good!" Jill exclaimed as Matt crossed home plate.

Kylie just nodded as she beamed with pride.

The next few innings went by slowly, with several pitching changes and no real offensive plays. Finally, several of Matt's teammates managed to get on base during the eighth inning.

As the fans were screaming for another home run, Matt bunted the ball and his teammate scored to put them ahead by one. Matt was thrown out, but the next batter got a hit to put them up another run.

When the game ended, the Grizzlies won 4–2.

As the crowd began to filter out of the stadium, Kylie just put her feet up on the seat in front of her. "We might as well wait here for a few minutes and let the crowd die down."

Jill nodded. "Good idea."

"Oh, look!" Leslie jumped up from her seat as Matt came out of the dugout and walked toward their section. "There's Matt."

Matt waved at Kylie to come to the railing, but Leslie assumed his signal was meant for her. Even as Leslie started toward the railing, Brooke stepped out in front of her and approached Matt.

"Hey, Matt," Brooke greeted him as Leslie stepped beside her.

"You were wonderful tonight," Leslie gushed.

"Thanks." Matt nodded toward the rest of their group, and then directed his comment to Brooke. "I need to go change, but I was thinking about going to get something to eat afterward."

"I'd love to," Leslie said as though Matt had asked her out exclusively.

Brooke bit her tongue before adding, "I'm sure everyone would like to go. Where do you want us to meet you?"

"I don't know how long I'll be." Matt glanced back at the team manager. "How about if we just meet at the diner over on Center Street?"

Leslie looked from Brooke to Matt, as though expecting him to uninvite everyone else.

"We'll see you there," Brooke told him and watched Matt jog back into the dugout.

Leslie turned on her before she could rejoin her roommates. "That was rude."

"Excuse me?" Brooke pushed her dark hair behind her ears and squared her shoulders so that she was facing Leslie straight on.

"Can't you find your own date?" Leslie demanded, her face flushing.

Brooke laughed in spite of herself. "Leslie, he was inviting everyone, not just you."

"Of course he invited everyone, since you came rushing over to see him. He didn't want to be rude."

"At least someone has some manners." Brooke turned and rejoined Jill and Kylie.

Kylie waited anxiously for Brooke to relay the conversation with Leslie. Once she, Brooke, and Jill were in Jill's car alone, Brooke described the whole conversation in detail.

"You know she's going to be hanging all over him tonight," Brooke told them as they pulled up in the parking lot of the diner.

"Matt looks like he can take care of himself," Kylie said as she stepped out of the car, noticing Leslie and the rest of their group already walking into the restaurant.

Jill just shook her head. "I hope so."

When they walked inside, the waitress was already pulling several tables together to make room for everyone. Leslie was trying to orchestrate where everyone would sit, claiming a seat in the center for herself and saving the seat next to her by placing her purse on it.

Even though Brooke had tried to get Kylie to sit on the other side of the seat Leslie was clearly saving for Matt, Kylie made herself content to sit at the end across from Garth.

As the group looked over their menus, their conversation centered around the game and Matt's obvious status as one of the best on the team. The companionable chatter ceased when Matt stepped through the door, and Leslie moved her purse from the seat next to her.

"Looks like the gang's all here." Matt pulled a chair from the empty table next to them and absentmindedly slid it to the head of the table by Kylie and Garth. Leslie could only gape as he sat down and took the menu Garth offered him.

"What is everyone getting? Dinner or dessert?" Matt asked over the top of his menu.

"I think we're settling on appetizers and dessert," Veronica told him.

Matt nodded, grateful when conversation picked up again at the far end of the table. He turned to Kylie and asked, "Did you want to split some nachos?"

"I think I'm going to stick with dessert," Kylie told him.

Matt just nodded as the waitress came to take their orders, beginning with Matt.

"I'll have the nachos, and she'll have a piece of cheesecake." Matt motioned to Kylie and handed his menu to the waitress.

Kylie bit her tongue as the waitress passed over her to take Brooke's order. She took several deep breaths, trying to calm herself. If Matt noticed how quiet she became, or that she barely touched her cheesecake when it arrived, he didn't comment on it.

An hour later, when they all loaded into their respective cars, it was Leslie who tried to get a ride with Matt, not Kylie. As usual, Caitlin rescued Matt from the awkward situation by insisting that Matt shouldn't have to go out of his way to take her home.

When Matt arrived at his apartment, he left the outside light on, hoping that Kylie would come over. He wanted to see her alone, but when he opened the door a short time later, Kylie wordlessly stepped into his apartment and closed the door behind her.

"Matt! What were you thinking?" Kylie put her hands on her hips, staring at him in frustration.

"What did I do?" he asked blankly.

"You didn't even ask what I wanted before you ordered for me." She took a deep breath. Keeping her voice controlled was taking considerable effort.

"You always get cheesecake for dessert." Matt held his hands up, bewildered. "If you wanted something else, you should have just said something."

"What I wanted isn't the issue."

"Then you *did* want cheesecake." Matt crossed his arms, convinced she was being completely irrational.

"Yes, I wanted cheesecake." Kylie stepped forward, grabbed his shirt, and pulled on it until they were eye to eye. She spoke slowly, carefully enunciating each word to make her point. "But how did you know that Kylie Ramsey likes cheesecake?"

Matt blinked, turned his head, and then looked her in the eye again. He lifted his hands up to hers and pried her fingers open so she would release his shirt. With a step backward, he blew out a long breath. "Okay, so I screwed up."

"Yeah." Kylie held her arms out to her sides. "Big-time."

"I'm sorry." Matt leaned against the back of his couch. "I just ordered automatically. I mean, you always expected me to order for you before."

"I know." Kylie's voice softened. "But we're on borrowed time right now. If I get relocated again, we'll be separated for who knows how long."

"I'm sorry," Matt repeated, his voice barely a whisper.

Tears came to Kylie's eyes. "I can't go through losing you again." She looked up into his eyes. "I just can't."

Slipping his arms around her, he pulled her into the warmth of his embrace. "Then you won't."

CHAPTER 9

"Are you going to tell us what's going on between you and Matt?" Brooke demanded as soon as Kylie walked in the door.

Kylie dropped her swim bag and ran her fingers through her damp hair. After seeing Matt, she had gone for a short swim, knowing that her roommates would notice if she came home completely dry.

"What are you talking about?" Kylie asked innocently.

"I mean, he goes out of his way to sit by you tonight." Brooke closed the textbook that was on the coffee table in front of her. "And then he orders for you."

Resigned that she would have to make some kind of excuse, Kylie dropped down on the couch.

"Brooke said he even knew what to order without asking you," Jill added.

"First of all, he knew I liked cheesecake because I said something about it at that cookout a while back." Kylie shrugged. "I was as shocked as you guys that he just ordered it for me. It was actually pretty rude of him."

"I don't know—" Jill started to defend him before Brooke cut her off.

"But he did deliberately sit by you instead of taking the only open seat at the table."

Kylie laughed. "Don't you think it would be more accurate to say that he deliberately *didn't* sit next to Leslie?"

Jill looked from Brooke to Kylie and back to Brooke. "She may have a point."

"No way." Brooke kicked her feet up on the table. "I know he likes Kylie."

Kylie stood up and collected her swim bag. "Well, I don't know if I want to go out with a guy that just assumes he knows what I want."

"Don't tell me he's already blown it and you haven't even been out on a date yet," Brooke moaned. "You two would make the perfect couple."

"Well, aren't you just the little matchmaker," Kylie said, letting some of her frustration with Matt spill over into the conversation.

Always the peacemaker, Jill spoke up. "She just wants you to be happy."

Kylie's stance softened. "I know. I just don't want you guys trying to set me up."

"Okay, okay." Brooke held her hands up in a gesture of peace. "But you would make a great couple."

* * *

Matt grinned to himself as he rang Kylie's doorbell. Brooke had invited him over for dinner to repay him for the tickets, and he had accepted as though he had no idea what she was up to.

Kylie had already told him about her roommates' attempt at matchmaking, and the fact that they had chosen him for her only made them more endearing. Since he knew Brooke would make sure Kylie was home for dinner, he had neglected to mention his invitation to her.

He had been prepared to walk in and see the shocked look on her face, but he hadn't really expected her to answer the door.

"Matt." Kylie hushed her voice. "What are you doing here?"

Poking his head inside and realizing that her roommates were still in the kitchen, he stole a quick kiss. Her eyes clouded with a mixture of pleasure and frustration as she looked nervously behind her.

"Aren't you going to invite me in?" Matt stepped past her into the apartment. "Mmm. Something sure smells good."

Jill was the first to poke her head out of the kitchen. "Hi, Matt. Come on in."

Brooke stepped into the living room and smiled at Kylie. "Kylie, why don't you entertain Matt for us until dinner is ready?"

Kylie noticed the mischievous look in Brooke's eyes. Realizing she had been set up, she asked wryly, "Are you sure you don't need any help?"

"No, no. You two just relax," Brooke insisted before disappearing back into the kitchen.

Matt held his hand out, waiting for Kylie to sit down.

She sat in the living room chair and kicked her feet up on the coffee table. "I'm surprised no one mentioned that you were coming over for dinner tonight."

Matt just shrugged his shoulders. "Do you like surprises?"

"Sometimes." Kylie shook her head, amusement quickly replacing annoyance. She couldn't stop staring at him, and seeing him here in her home made his presence in Texas just that much more real.

"Dinner's ready," Jill called from the kitchen, carrying the casserole to the table.

Everyone sat down, and Brooke silently congratulated herself when Matt ended up next to Kylie.

"So, Matt, are you going to the dance on Saturday?" Brooke asked with a hint in her voice as she looked from him to Kylie.

"I'm thinking about it." Matt let Brooke suffer for a minute before adding, "I have a game that afternoon, so I'm not sure if I'll be able to make it in time."

"Oh," Brooke muttered, visibly disappointed.

"Are all of you going?" Matt asked, suppressing a grin.

"We're planning on it." Jill glanced at Kylie. "Kylie has to go because she's on the decorating committee."

Kylie glared at Jill and Brooke before explaining to Matt, "They signed me up when I wasn't there."

Matt laughed. "Well, if I make it to the dance, I'll help you with the cleanup anyway."

"We never have enough people for that part of the job," Kylie told him as though they hadn't already had this conversation. She knew perfectly well that his game was scheduled to end about the time the dance started, and he expected to be about an hour late getting to it.

As they all finished off the ice cream Jill served for dessert, Kylie rose from the table. "Since you guys cooked, I guess it's my turn to clean up."

"I'll give you a hand." Matt collected everyone's dirty dishes and followed Kylie into the kitchen.

Kylie didn't bother discouraging him from helping. She knew firsthand that while he rarely did dishes in his own apartment, preferring paper plates to real ones, Matt would feel uncomfortable just sitting around while everyone waited on him. Kylie tossed a towel at him as she slid the dirty dishes into the sink. Brooke and Jill cleared the rest of the dishes from the table and put away the leftovers.

"Oh, no!" Brooke said as she put the last of the food into the refrigerator.

"What's wrong?" Kylie asked, turning from the sink.

"I just forgot to pick up a book I needed from the library." She looked apologetic as she turned to Jill. "Jill, I hate to ask, but could you run me over there?"

"Sure." Jill grabbed her keys, which were lying conveniently on the kitchen counter. "Matt, I'm sorry we have to rush out like this."

"No problem." Matt dried the dish in his hand as he glanced at Kylie, who was trying desperately to keep a straight face. "Thanks for dinner."

"Anytime." Jill rushed out of the apartment with Brooke at her heels.

The door had barely closed when Kylie and Matt both burst out laughing. "A book from the library?" Kylie choked.

"They really could have come up with a better excuse than that." Matt's laughter stopped, and he set down the dish he was holding. "I've never been alone with you in your apartment before."

Kylie held up the spatula she was holding and aimed it at him. "Behave."

"Who, me?" Matt grabbed the spatula out of her hand and enveloped her in his arms. His eyes were teasing when he asked, "Don't you trust me?"

"No, I don't." Kylie put both hands on his chest and tried to push away. She might as well have been shoving at a mountain. "I know you better than anyone thinks I know you."

"Kylie . . ." Matt said, still adjusting to the feel of her new name on his lips. "I don't know why you don't trust me."

"Don't even . . ."

He was tickling her before she could finish her sentence.

"Matt!" she squealed, trying to wriggle away from him.

"What's wrong?" Matt's fingers continued to play on her stomach as she gasped for breath.

"Stop!" Kylie finally dug her teeth into his shoulder.

"Ouch." Matt pulled back, laughter still in his eyes. "You bit me."

"You tickled me." Kylie pushed free of his arms. "You know how ticklish I am."

The grin spread across his face. "Yeah."

"Matt, I'm warning you." Kylie backed out of the kitchen and raced into the living room. She had hoped to make it to the hallway, but he was too quick for her. Snagging one arm around her waist, Matt picked her up and dumped her unceremoniously on the couch.

"Of course, if you don't want to be tickled . . ." Matt knelt down next to her and took her face in his hands.

The laughter in Kylie's eyes clouded like a storm brewing on the horizon as Matt leaned closer. He brushed his lips against hers gently. As she caught her breath, Matt just stared down at her.

"Do you have any idea how hard it is to keep from coming over here to see you every day?" Matt asked.

Kylie nodded. "I've had that same problem since I found out where you live."

"What are we going to do about it?" Matt sat down on the couch next to her, taking her hand, studying the way it fit so neatly into his.

Kylie shrugged. "At least we get to talk on the phone every day. Besides, it's not like you have a lot of time between your practices and games."

"Still, talking on the phone for five minutes when your roommates aren't around isn't exactly what I had in mind for a relationship."

"I know," Kylie sighed, wondering what would happen if they dated publicly. "We'll see each other at the dance at least."

"I think it's about time I staked my claim," Matt told her.

Kylie's eyebrows shot up. "Oh, really?"

"I know you've managed to avoid dating other people this past year, and I've sure done my best to keep my few dates at arm's length." Matt took a deep breath and let it out slowly. "I want something more. I want to be able to call you up and ask how your day is going. I don't want to feel like I have to sneak around to be a part of your life."

"What if they find us?" Kylie asked softly. "It's not safe for you to be with me."

"You know I wouldn't come anywhere near you if I thought Rush still had people watching me." Matt's hand tightened on hers. "Secret Service followed me around right up until a few months before I moved here. They hadn't found anything suspicious in over six months."

"Even if Rush's men aren't watching you, we still have to worry about Doug."

"That's what you're really worried about, isn't it?"

Kylie nodded. "I meant what I said the other night about not wanting to lose you again. But I also don't want to lose the friends I've made here."

"Jill and Brooke are pretty terrific."

"Except for you, they're the only close friends I've had since . . ." Kylie swallowed hard. "Since Chase died."

Matt stood and stepped away. "Doug obviously doesn't realize I'm living here, or he would have shown up by now." He turned to face her. "And whether we are dating or not, if he realizes it, the result is going to be the same."

Kylie nodded. "You're probably right."

"So, can we start being a couple?"

"I really think we should torment my roommates a little longer." A grin spread across her face. "But if you were to sweep me off my feet at the dance and ask me out, I might say yes."

"Just promise me you'll stick with me at the dance," Matt pleaded. "I can't stand the thought of getting cornered by Leslie."

Kylie giggled before leaning over to kiss him. "You'd better get going before my roommates get home and find out you're still here."

"You're going to tell them I left right after they did, aren't you?"

"Yep." Kylie grinned.

CHAPTER 10

The music had been blaring for more than an hour, and Kylie stood by the refreshment table watching new couples forming by the minute. The lights were dimmed, and a disco ball was hanging from the ceiling. Streamers and balloons attempted unsuccessfully to hide the fact that the dance was being held in the cultural hall. Even the basketball hoops were draped with streamers.

Kylie glanced down at her watch for the third time in five minutes, scolding herself for being so anxious. After picking up another glass of punch, she realized that she had already consumed far too much. She set her glass back down on the table and went out into the hallway. As she neared the restroom, voices carried toward her. She heard her name just before she rounded the corner.

". . . odd that Kylie of all people was sitting right next to us at the game?" Leslie's voice was accusing, though Kylie wasn't sure exactly what she was being accused of.

"Matt must have given her and her roommates tickets too," a voice that sounded like Veronica's said casually.

"Well, if he's interested in Kylie, it's only because she looks like his old girlfriend," Leslie insisted. "It shouldn't take him long to figure out that Kylie never dates anyway."

"I don't know what you have against her." Annoyance laced Veronica's voice. "It's not like she's ever done anything to you."

"Didn't you see the way she was with Matt after the game?" Leslie whined. "I mean, she was acting like they were an item or something."

"Leslie, she didn't do anything," Veronica insisted. "What did you expect her to do? Stand up and tell him not to sit by her?"

"She could have pointed out that there was still an empty seat at the table."

"One of these days you're going to have to grow up and realize that guys can make up their own minds about who they date," Veronica's voice snapped. "I'm tired of you telling everyone who they can and can't be interested in because you always want to stake a claim first. You can be so possessive."

Veronica was shaking her head in disgust as she came around the corner. She glanced up apologetically when she saw Kylie and continued down the hall.

Kylie waited a minute before rounding the corner into the restroom. She wished she had waited longer when she opened the door to find Leslie with a handful of tissues in her hand and tears streaming down her cheeks.

"Are you okay?" Kylie forced herself to ask, preparing for Leslie's famous dramatics.

"Veronica and I just had a fight," Leslie whimpered, wiping away the mascara that was pooling under her eyes.

"I'm sorry." Kylie ducked into a bathroom stall, hoping that some other poor soul would come in and give Leslie a shoulder to cry on, but when she came back out a minute later, Leslie was still standing there alone.

"Do you think I'm possessive?" Leslie asked, still wiping at her running mascara.

Kylie swallowed. "Excuse me?"

"Of guys." Leslie pushed her hair behind her shoulders. "I can't help the way I look."

"Leslie, you are very beautiful. Everyone knows that." Kylie hesitated, looking for the right words. "I guess I don't know why you don't just let the guys come to you. Everyone knows they would if you gave them the chance."

"You think I chase after guys?" Leslie asked, her voice tense.

Kylie shook her head, wishing she had just turned and run out of the bathroom when she had the chance. "I think when a beautiful woman even hints that she's interested in a guy, it scares him off. What might work for the rest of us doesn't always work for someone who is pretty enough to be a model."

Leslie tapped a finger to her chin, considering. "Maybe if I played hard to get, Matt would ask me out."

Kylie winced inwardly. "Why are you so determined to go out with Matt?"

"Because he's the guy *everyone* wants to go out with," Leslie admitted.

"Maybe you should worry less about being the envy of everyone and more about who would be fun for you to be with," Kylie suggested. "I'm going to go back into the dance."

"Would you wait for me?" Leslie asked, her voice unusually sincere. "I don't want to go back in by myself."

Kylie fought the urge to glance at her watch and nodded. "Sure."

Leslie touched up her makeup amazingly fast and followed Kylie back out into the hall. When they entered the dance, Matt was still nowhere in sight, but Kylie noticed Garth staring at Leslie and then looking away flushed.

Kylie leaned closer to Leslie. "Do you want to really make someone's night?"

"Whose?"

"I think Garth would think he was in heaven if you asked him to dance," Kylie told her. "He was just staring at you when we came in."

"Really?" Leslie glanced over at Garth, who was trying hard not to look their direction. "I've known him forever, and he's never acted like he was interested in me."

"Maybe he was just afraid to tell you," Kylie suggested. "Worst case is you end up sharing a couple of dances with a good friend."

A genuine smile crossed Leslie's face. "You're right."

* * *

Matt stared at them together—Leslie and Kylie talking like they were best friends. He couldn't believe his eyes when Leslie gave Kylie a hug before crossing the room toward him. A dozen excuses raced through his mind as he anticipated her asking him to dance.

Matt just stood there in a stupor when she said hello and walked right by. With a glance over his shoulder, he saw Leslie stop to talk to Garth. Amazed, he crossed the room to Kylie.

"What was that?" Matt asked, leaning over so she could hear him over the noise.

"Leslie's had a rough night," Kylie informed him.

The music slowed, and Matt instinctively took her hand. "Do you want to dance?"

Kylie nodded, letting him lead her onto the dance floor. Matt caught her smile and followed her gaze to where Garth and Leslie were already dancing together.

As he took Kylie into his arms, Matt breathed in her scent. The fragrance of raspberries from her shampoo still scented her hair, mixing with the smell of the lotion she used religiously to counteract the effects of hours in the pool.

Through her light cotton dress, he could feel the definition of the muscles in her back as he twirled her around the dance floor. He never would have guessed that someone so slight could possess such strength had he not seen her in the water.

He had held her in his arms many times before, but this was their first dance together. Of course, when they had dated before, she had always shied away from crowds. Looking down at her now, Matt realized how much she had changed over the past year. Not only was she more comfortable with herself, but she seemed more comfortable around others as well.

Though he wanted to lean down and tell her about his game and the antics of some of his teammates, he was all too aware of their surroundings. The easy conversation that had always been central to their relationship would give away as much as a kiss would. The speculative glances would turn to gossip by the end of the evening, and while Matt wanted the world to know that his heart belonged to her, he knew it needed to appear as though he and Kylie were just beginning a relationship.

Kylie started to step away when the song ended, but Matt held her firmly in his arms as another slow song began.

"Where do you think you're going?" he teased. "One dance isn't enough to stake a claim."

Kylie's eyebrows shot up. "Oh, really? What would your mother think if she heard you talking like that?"

"Are you kidding?" Matt laughed. "She'd be thrilled to know that I'm interested in dating again, especially someone she would approve of."

Kylie smiled in response. "She might approve under normal circumstances. I'm not so sure that she would want you dating me, though."

"We both know better than that." Of all of the girls he had brought home over the years, his parents had never accepted anyone so quickly. They had recognized immediately what Matt had just been discovering at the time. Kylie brought out the best in him and, by so doing, showed him more happiness than he had ever thought possible.

Matt kept Kylie on the dance floor for the better part of an hour until he finally led her to the punch bowl, where she had started her evening. As some friends joined them, both Matt and Kylie ended up on the dance floor with new partners, but when the final song was announced, they found each other once again.

Everyone groaned collectively when the lights came back to full strength and the magic of the evening faded into memory. Within minutes, the diligent few who had volunteered to clean up were clearing away the decorations in the cultural hall.

Kylie worked on putting away the refreshments while Matt wrestled with the industrial-strength vacuum cleaner. Jill and Brooke had remained behind, feeling somewhat guilty for volunteering Kylie when she wasn't around.

As the cleanup crew started to leave the building, Kylie tied up the garbage bag in the kitchen and hauled it outside, leaving Jill to finish mopping the floor. She scanned the darkness, listening intently for a moment before stepping outside. Kylie had just reached the dark corner of the parking lot where the dumpster was located when she turned suddenly at the sound of footsteps, her heart pounding.

"What are you doing?" Matt demanded, emerging from the shadows.

"Taking out the garbage." Kylie struggled to lift the large bag. Matt took it from her and heaved it effortlessly into the dumpster.

"You shouldn't be out here by yourself," Matt insisted. His voice took on an edge as he added, "I would think that you of all people would be more careful."

"Excuse me?" Kylie looked at him incredulously.

"What if someone were out here?" Matt motioned to the trees behind the dumpster, pointing out the seclusion of this particular part of the parking lot. "No one would even know where you were."

Fear edged to the surface from where Kylie had buried it deep inside her. It battled with her temper as she faced Matt. "Jill knew I was out here."

"That's not the point. You could be gone before Jill suspected anything was wrong."

How could she tell him that she deliberately didn't think about what might happen? Could he even begin to understand her need to keep fear from dominating her life? "You think I'm not capable of taking out the garbage by myself?" Kylie asked through clenched teeth.

"Not in the middle of the night," Matt snapped.

"You know, it seems to me that I did just fine before you moved here." Kylie stepped closer, keeping her eyes on his. "And I don't remember ever needing your permission to perform such a mundane task."

"It's not a matter of permission." Matt shook his head, grasping for the right words. "How can I protect you if you're going to be this careless?"

Kylie's eyes darkened. "I didn't ask for your *protection*. I refuse to live the rest of my life always looking over my shoulder."

"I guess I just assumed you had a little more common sense than this." Matt stepped back. "Sorry for caring."

Kylie's temper was replaced by a sharp doubt. "Maybe it's not me you really care about. Maybe you expect me to live up to your memory of somebody else."

As Matt stared at her, Kylie fought back the tears that threatened to surface. Unable to speak, she turned and walked away, wondering how such a wonderful evening could have ended so badly.

He saw the tears glistening in her eyes, and he wanted to rush after her. His feet just wouldn't move. He could only watch as Jill and Brooke joined her outside and Kylie drove away with them.

Slowly, he crossed the parking lot to his own car. How had this happened? Wasn't she still the same girl he had fallen in love with not so long ago? As he drove home, he was forced to admit that even though he had noticed changes in her, he still thought of her as Shaye. Even the name Kylie was foreign to him.

As he opened the door to his apartment and flipped on the light, the stranger on the wall stared back at him. The nervousness and underlying vulnerability that had first intrigued him were buried deep inside the woman who had become Kylie Ramsey. Shaye would have never walked into a dark parking lot alone. And he had never known she possessed the temper that had raged at him tonight.

Exhausted, Matt tried to go straight to bed, but sleep wouldn't come. Less than an hour after he had arrived home, he was clearing off his cluttered drawing table. After situating his art supplies, Matt picked up his pencil and allowed his feelings to take over.

Throughout the early morning hours, his pencil was replaced with charcoals, and his bed became littered with artwork. As he rubbed his hands over his face, barely noticing the stubble that had appeared during the night, light began streaming through the window.

He knelt by his bed, shuffling the sketches he had drawn. As he looked into the eyes of the woman he had drawn, he saw someone entirely different than the sketches he had drawn of her so many months before.

He was amazed that these new drawings were every bit as compelling as the ones that had earned him his first art award. They were of Kylie, not Shaye. The fear that had always been buried just under the surface had been replaced with a simple caution and a steely determination. The humor that had so rarely surfaced before was now a more ready part of her. And the loneliness was gone.

Did she still need him now that she had found herself? Without him, she had already testified in court more than a dozen times, learned to deal with the constant threat against her life, and found contentment in the life she had made for herself here. Was there still room for him?

As Matt thought of the man who had loved her before, he wondered if Chase would even recognize her now, had he lived. He hung his head and poured out his heart in prayer. The questions came fast and furiously. Was his future with Kylie? Or was he in love with an image he had created over the past year that was a combination of his dreams and reality? Had he just been intrigued by the secret she guarded so closely when he first saw her almost eighteen months before, or was the love he felt for her strong enough to last an eternity? And had the Lord brought them together again so their relationship could progress, or were they supposed to realize that they were never meant to be?

His heart was still heavy as he rose from his bedside and started to get ready for church. As he sat alone during sacrament meeting, he remembered the feeling that had come over him the first time he sat next to her in the chapel.

She had listened so intently to everything the speakers said that day, often following along in her worn scriptures. He knew that sitting next to her in church, without a word passing between them, had been the moment he had fallen in love with her.

Her fragile state of mind and his need to be strong for her had not been an issue then. Thinking of their argument last night, he knew that it had resulted from the physical distance between them the past year. Maybe he was still in love with a memory, but he knew that didn't exclude the possibility of being in love with the person she had become.

The hope he had rekindled during the three hours of meetings was doused when he exited the building. He caught a glimpse of her across the parking lot as she made her way to another entrance. She lifted her head when she sensed his presence, and, without a backward glance, continued into the building as though he had never been part of her life.

CHAPTER 11

The first long road trip for Matt's baseball team couldn't have been timed any worse. Matt had tried the night before they left to catch Kylie at home but had been unsuccessful. Since her roommates had been out too, he hadn't even been able to leave a message. He had finally resorted to calling her cell phone, surprised to get her voice mail instead of her. At a loss for words, he hung up rather than trying to talk to a machine.

The thought of spending the better part of two weeks on a bus traveling from one city to another held even less appeal now. The first several games were scheduled at night, and Matt wasn't able to call Kylie again until they had been on the road a week.

Jill answered the first time he called. Brooke answered the next two. But Kylie was never home. Extra swim practices had been the usual excuse. Matt finally left messages on her cell phone's voice mail and wasn't surprised that his calls weren't returned. He could only hope that she was in the pool trying to work out her own frustrations the way he was doing with a baseball bat.

Matt already knew what it was like to miss her, but he had never expected to feel so alone without her. Before moving to Texas, he had friends and family to rely on. Now he realized how much he had come to rely on just hearing her voice and words of encouragement every day.

With his emotions so close to the surface, Matt had expected to play poorly when they had set out for their first long stretch of away games for spring training. The home run he hit during his first at-bat was more of a surprise to him than to the pitcher, who had been on the verge of striking him out. Throughout the road trip, he had continued to abuse the baseball whenever he stepped into the batter's box.

Even a major league scout had stopped to talk to him, though Matt didn't hold any real stock in the possibilities he had offered. After growing up around politics, he didn't believe any promises until he saw them in writing.

When he finally returned home, he was grateful for his own bed and the chance to mend fences with Kylie. When his phone calls continued to go unanswered, he decided it would take more extreme measures to get through to her.

* * *

The first week she hadn't heard from him just proved what she had discovered so rudely the night of the dance. Matt wasn't who she thought he was. By the time the phone calls started, her anger had already peaked.

She had been kicking herself for shutting out any possibility of even the most casual dates with boys from the stake during the past year. Her memories of being with Matt had been so sweet that she had been certain they would find a future together once this business with Chris Rush was over.

But the sweet, gentle man she had fallen in love with had turned into an overprotective, thickheaded jock who thought he could run her life. Well, he could just find some Barbie doll to play the role of the baseball player's girlfriend.

When the doorbell rang, she just waited for one of her roommates to answer it. She had avoided answering both the door and the phone for the past few weeks, grateful that Brooke and Jill had not pressed her for information about Matt. Her stormy mood after the dance had been enough to warn them not to bring up his name.

"Oh, my!" Jill's voice carried through the apartment. "Thank you so much."

Kylie forced herself to stay seated at the kitchen table where she was organizing her notes. The smell of flowers had her looking up when Jill walked in with a huge basket.

A spray of daisies smiled from the middle of the basket, and an assortment of individually wrapped muffins encircled the flowers.

"Blast him," Kylie muttered under her breath.

Jill just raised an eyebrow when she drew out the card and extended it to Kylie. "It's for you."

Kylie snatched the card and tossed it onto the table unopened. "Thanks."

"Who was at the door?" Brooke asked, walking into the kitchen. "Oh, wow."

"At least read the card," Jill suggested.

"I don't want to read the card." Kylie stood up from the table, annoyance edging her voice. "I'm going to swim."

Brooke watched Kylie stalk down the hall. "Doesn't she even want to know who they're from?"

"She knows who they're from," Jill informed her. "And I bet we could figure it out on our first guess."

"Matt?" Brooke asked hopefully.

"It has to be." Jill settled down into a chair. "She's been grumpy ever since that dance."

Brooke and Jill just watched as Kylie strode back down the hall toward them. She started to pass through the kitchen, hesitating by the table. With a huff, she grabbed a blueberry muffin from the basket and stormed out of the apartment.

"I never thought I'd see her fall for anybody so fast." Jill shook her head, amazed.

"And they haven't even been out on a date yet."

* * *

Matt waited in the college parking lot, hoping he could still predict her moods. He glanced at his watch. The basket should have been delivered at least fifteen minutes ago. She should have gotten here by now . . .

He grinned as he saw her park her car on the far side of the parking lot. She got out and slammed her car door, swinging her swim bag over her shoulder. Her determined stride toward the aquatics building kept him in his car for a few minutes longer. When he was sure she would already be in the pool, Matt got out of his car and found a seat on a bench a few yards from where Kylie was swimming the breaststroke.

Oh, she's plenty mad, he thought to himself, suppressing a grin. He bet she didn't even read the card before she went storming out of her apartment.

When she swam several individual medleys in succession, Matt wondered if he had misread her mood. Though he loved to see her swim the different strokes, especially the butterfly, he knew she always reverted to breaststroke when she was really upset. He had just never had that anger directed at him before.

He settled back to watch her, smiling when she switched to breaststroke again. When they had said good-bye before Kylie had been relocated here, Matt never would have guessed that he would miss seeing her swim. Yet he loved seeing her in the water—the beautiful strokes, the strength and determination, the dedication to continue to improve. He watched for more than an hour, breathing a sigh of relief when she finally switched to freestyle for her cooldown.

Fingering the thick, oversized towel he had bought her on his trip, he stood and walked to the end of her lane. She didn't even see him until she jumped out of the pool, spilling water onto the deck.

He moved quickly, wrapping her in the towel before she could react. The towel almost reached her ankles, and she shivered as Matt rubbed his hands over her arms to dry them.

"I'm not even going to ask what you're doing here," Kylie muttered, turning for the locker room.

Matt just watched her go, leaving the pool area for the parking lot. He was waiting by her car when she emerged from the building.

"What do you want from me?" Kylie dropped her bag on the ground and held her hands out in frustration. "I can't be the person you want me to be."

"Maybe I'll like the new you better," Matt suggested.

Her hands fisted as she placed them on her hips. "I can tell you that I liked the old you better."

"How do you know? We had a fast, intense relationship when we first met. Maybe it would have burned out had we kept going the way we started. Don't you think we should get to know each other as we are now?"

"You're possessive, self-centered, controlling . . ." Kylie's temper flashed. "Why would I want to know more?"

"Because I'm good to my mother, I love animals, especially horses, and I find you an absolutely intriguing subject to sketch."

"The person you loved to sketch doesn't exist anymore." Kylie stepped closer, ignoring the smell of his cologne. "I couldn't let her."

"Why?" Matt noticed the determination in her eyes, another first.

Anger snapped in her voice. "I got tired of letting fear rule my life. It's a lousy way to live, and I won't do it again."

"Let me get to know you." Matt kept his distance, though he ached to take her hand, touch her cheek, anything to put them in physical contact.

"I'll think about it." Kylie disengaged her car alarm and tossed her bag into the passenger seat.

"How about lunch tomorrow?" Matt suggested, placing a hand on her shoulder before she could climb into the car. "Say one o'clock?"

Kylie shook her head. "I don't think so."

Matt just watched her drive away, determined that he would get through to her.

* * *

Yellow carnations came with the New York–style cheesecake. Red roses accompanied the chocolates from See's Candies. But it was the Easter lilies that came in a simple crystal vase that undid her.

Each day as she sat in class, she fought to keep her mind on the subject at hand as Matt kept crowding her thoughts. More than once, her professors had caught her wondering absently what Matt would send next.

She knew she was softening toward him again, not so much because of the gifts but because of the thought that inspired them. She supposed it was simple enough for him to remember her favorite breakfast food and her favorite dessert. She also remembered mentioning once that See's Candies was one of the things she missed from home. Of course, that conversation had taken place nearly two years ago. It might have even been coincidence that the only time she had been given Easter lilies was by her father just months before he died.

Now that her anger was wearing off—and Kylie found it was taking too much of her energy to maintain it anyway—she had to admit that Matt knew her better than anyone. More, he still remembered how to be her friend, even though she was making that practically impossible.

She hadn't seen him for almost a week except for a glimpse of him on the evening news. Though the media had obviously not made the connection between Matt and his father, his skills on the baseball field had his celebrity status increasing as the opening day of the regular season approached. In addition to the handful of home runs and stolen bases he had accumulated, Matt had also already demonstrated his ability to play both first base and right field.

When she opened the card that accompanied the lilies, she was surprised when something fell out of it. Leaning over, she picked up three tickets to the season opener. Inside the card Matt had written simply, "Please come to the game. I really need to know I have a friend in the stands."

Kylie smiled down at the tickets in her hand, noticing that he had automatically given her tickets for Jill and Brooke. The simple note warmed her heart more than any of the gifts he had sent her, reminding her once again of the friendship they had once shared. Shrugging her shoulders, she walked down the hall in search of her roommates. After all, he had always been there for her.

CHAPTER 12

They found their seats easily, the same ones they had occupied during the previous game they had attended. Kylie smiled to herself when she saw that the rest of the gang had already arrived, except this time they had all shifted seats. Leslie was nestled next to Garth as he patiently explained the batting order.

Veronica passed a box of popcorn to Kylie, winking at her as she glanced back at Leslie. Kylie returned her smile and shared the popcorn with her roommates. She was scanning the field for Matt when a couple started down their row, trying to make their way to the empty seats next to her.

She stood to let them by, her eyes on the field. It wasn't until she sat back down that she glanced at the woman seated next to her. Their eyes met, and both of them gasped.

Kylie was looking into the eyes of Katherine Whitmore, Matt's mother. Her dark hair was pulled back in a simple ponytail, giving her an even more youthful look than Kylie remembered. Shock and surprise showed on the strong, beautiful face, but the woman's emotions were only visible for a moment. Katherine's fine-tuned ability to appear calm in any setting took over, and she quickly regained her dignified yet friendly composure.

In a subtle move, Katherine nudged her husband. The older version of Matt smiled down at his wife automatically before his eyes followed hers to land on Kylie. Senator Jim Whitmore did a double take, his gaze turning to a hard stare.

Panic filled Kylie as a terrifying thought struck her. What if Matt's parents told Doug that they had seen her? Suddenly her reservations about dating Matt seemed absurd as she realized how foolish she had been. How would she ever know if she and Matt had a future together if she wouldn't even give him the chance to get to know who she was now?

Flustered, Kylie looked away, grateful that her roommates were deep in conversation with their friends behind them.

The fact that Matt's parents would travel the distance from Virginia to Texas to come to one of his games surprised Kylie, though she knew it shouldn't have. When she had first visited the Whitmores' home in Virginia, she had envied their closeness and the way each family member supported the others. Such little things had caught her attention: the way Katherine held on a little longer than expected when hugging her children; the laughter so often heard when Matt was with his brother and sister; even the fact that Jim regularly put his family before the demands of his profession and the Washington social scene.

Jim and Katherine Whitmore had gone out of their way to make her feel welcome during her visit so long ago. She had even dared to hope that someday she might have a family of her own and be the kind of mother Katherine was. Her mind raced, knowing that this couple she so admired had the power to change her life once again.

Veronica was the first to notice Matt jogging onto the field. "Oh, there he is!"

Kylie turned her eyes to the field and watched him, her emotions mixed. Just the sight of him still caused her pulse to race, but she knew that they needed time to get to know each other again. Both of them had changed in ways that the other was still unfamiliar with.

Even as she considered that he might not be what she needed, her heart ached. With his parents sitting next to her, the realization that the FBI could separate them again became very real.

"Are you kids here to watch Matt?" Jim's voice cut through her thoughts.

Caitlin, who was sitting behind Kylie, nodded.

"Isn't that wonderful," Katherine commented, apparently unruffled at seeing Kylie. "We're his parents."

"Oh, it's so nice to meet you." Caitlin extended her hand to Katherine. "Matt didn't tell us you were coming."

"Actually, we just flew out today to surprise him," Jim said as a knowing look passed between him and Kylie.

As the game began, introductions were exchanged. Kylie was barely able to get her name out without stuttering.

As they all settled back to watch the game, Katherine patted Kylie's arm. "Do you go to school here in Texas, Kylie?"

Kylie nodded and prayed silently for strength. "Yes, I'm a sophomore."

"What are you studying?"

Her eyes were cool as she answered, "Criminal procedure."

Katherine just nodded as she looked back to the field where her son had just caught the ball to make an out at first base.

Kylie did her best to cheer with her friends for Matt and his team, but her stomach was tied in knots, and a panic she hadn't felt in months overwhelmed her. The old impulse to constantly survey her surroundings had resurfaced, as she sat on the edge of her seat, ready to spring.

Matt played well, making it onto base three times during the game and crossing home plate twice. After the game, he made his way to the stands, evidently searching for Kylie.

His mouth dropped open when he spotted her sitting right next to his parents. His plans to convince Kylie to go out with him after the game took a backseat to the explanation his parents would most certainly demand. As he watched Kylie leaving with her roommates, he could only wonder if she would ever open her heart to him again.

* * *

"Matt, what were you thinking?" Jim threw his hands up as he paced his son's apartment."

"I can't believe you just ran into her," Katherine added, wringing her hands together. "You know you should have told us about this."

"How was I supposed to do that?" Matt asked, then scolded himself for raising his voice at his parents. "We all learned the hard way how easy it is to tap phone lines and intercept mail. If I had told you, I would have been announcing where she is."

"This is just all so unsettling." Katherine made her way into the kitchen, hoping to find a task to occupy her hands.

"I know the Lord's hand is in this." Matt tried to keep his voice calm. "The chances that we would just accidentally run into each other are practically zero."

Jim ignored him, already focused on the next point he intended to make. "Look, you're becoming a household name around here with the success you've had in the preseason. Being with you is too risky for her right now."

"And being with her is too risky for you," Katherine added, remembering all too vividly the wound her son suffered the last time he had rushed to her aid.

"Believe it or not, she is hardly speaking to me at the moment." Matt collapsed onto the couch, surprised at how much that admission hurt.

Jim studied him for a moment and then sat across from him. "What happened?"

"She's changed." Matt shrugged. "I guess we both have."

Katherine carried two mugs of hot chocolate into the living room, handing one to her husband and the other to her son. "Everybody changes over time, especially during those early adult years."

"She's still awfully young, isn't she?" Jim asked.

"She's four years younger than me, barely twenty." Matt nodded. "Too young to go through all of this."

"Maybe your feelings for each other when you first dated were intensified because of the circumstances at the time," Katherine suggested.

"She seems to think I'm in love with an image I've created of her."

"Is she right?" Jim asked bluntly.

"I don't know. Maybe." Matt rubbed his face with his hands. "But it doesn't change the fact that I'm still in love with her. I want to know who she is now. She just doesn't want to let me."

"Rush's trial is set for this summer," Jim pointed out. "After that, you'll have the time to really get to know each other if that's what you both want."

"And how many times have they moved the trial back?" Matt stood, pacing off his frustration. "She thinks Rush will keep trying to push everything back until after the Olympic trials, hoping that his men can find her there."

"I really think we should let Doug Valdez know that you're living here," Jim insisted. "Just living near her could be putting both of you in danger."

"Dad, what are the chances that we would just accidentally run into each other like this?" Matt asked, hoping his father had calmed down enough to listen. "I don't know if she looks at it this way, but I know the Lord brought us together again. I just don't know why yet."

"Is that what your prayers have told you?" Katherine asked quietly.

Matt nodded, annoyed at the tears forming in his eyes.

"Then we'll have to trust you on this." Katherine hugged her son. "But promise you'll always listen for the Spirit to guide you."

"I promise."

* * *

Kylie sat in her car outside of Matt's apartment, trying to work up her nerve to go inside. She didn't know if his parents would be there, but she was preparing for the worst.

Instinctively, she glanced around the parking lot. Mustering all of her courage, she stepped out of the car and approached his door. It took another minute before she actually forced herself to ring the doorbell.

When Matt pulled the door open, he smiled wearily. "Come on in."

Kylie tried to look past him to see if he was alone, and Matt just shrugged. "They left twenty minutes ago," he said as he waited for her to step inside before closing the door behind her.

"Matt, what were you thinking?" Kylie threw her arms up in the air, and Matt bit the inside of his cheek to keep from laughing. He could feel a replay of his conversation with his parents coming on.

"I think I mailed my parents season tickets when I first moved here, figuring I didn't have anyone else to give them to." Matt sat on the couch and motioned for her to join him. "I had no idea they were coming when I sent the other tickets to you."

Kylie sat down next to him, leaving plenty of space between them. She ran her fingers through her hair and shook her head. "This isn't happening."

"What are you afraid of?" Matt asked, hoping that his parents' decision to keep their secret would be as great a relief to her as it was to him.

"I just don't want to start over again."

"Why?" Matt asked, hoping for the answer he wanted.

Kylie glared at him. "You don't know what it's like to have to start over without anyone to rely on but yourself." She stood and paced the room in a fair imitation of his father just a short while ago. "You still have a family and friends and you know what your name is going to be when you wake up in the morning."

"I am very fortunate to have a great family." Matt nodded. "And back home, I did have a lot of good friends." He stood and crossed the room, not stopping until he was standing just a breath away from her. "But you're wrong about one thing. I do know what it's like to be alone. I've felt that way a lot since moving here."

Kylie looked up and saw the loneliness in his eyes. Guilt washed over her as she realized how selfish she had been. "I could have made things easier on you here."

"Maybe." Matt shrugged. "I didn't want you to risk your new life here any more than you did."

"But I never even thought about how hard it must be for you to be living so far away from home, not really knowing anyone." She forced herself to look him in the eyes once more. "I guess I haven't exactly changed for the better since we saw each other last."

"I wouldn't say that." Matt shook his head and stepped back. Her scent was clouding his judgment, and he needed to put distance between them. "You were living in constant fear when we first met, even though I didn't understand why at the time."

"But even when I couldn't be honest with you, you were always there for me," Kylie said softly.

"I guess I'll have to adjust to you not needing my protection." Matt motioned to the sketch hanging on the wall. "You aren't that girl anymore."

"But do you know who I am now?" Kylie asked quietly.

Matt turned toward his room and reappeared holding a stack of sketches. "Why don't you tell me?"

Kylie looked at him curiously, following him to the kitchen table, where he spread out his latest series of drawings. They were of her.

Some were a combination of the girl she had been when they first met and the woman she was becoming, but they were definitely her.

As she shuffled through the papers, one sketch caught her eye. It seemed to depict her as she was yesterday, last year, and three years ago. He had sketched her head-on as she took a breath while swimming the breaststroke. Her shoulders were bunched as she prepared to thrust her arms forward, and behind the goggles, her eyes were focused straight ahead.

"I had forgotten how talented you are."

Matt folded his long legs and he sat in a chair, leaning his elbows on the table. "These are the first drawings I've done since I lost you."

"Why?" Kylie reached out, touched his arm, and sat beside him.

"I won the Rease Art Award with that first sketch I did of you." Matt's eyes focused on the far wall, and then he looked back at Kylie. "I was afraid I would never be able to create anything that good again."

Kylie motioned to the drawings on the table. "But these are wonderful."

"You inspire me." Matt lifted his hand and caressed her cheek. "When I lost you, I locked away that part of me."

"Is that why you decided to play baseball?" Kylie asked softly. "You were afraid you wouldn't succeed in graduate school?"

"I wasn't sure I still wanted to go to graduate school." Matt took her hand, placing his palm against hers. "I didn't know what I wanted for my future. When I prayed about my career options, nothing felt right until I was offered the chance to play baseball. I guess I wasn't ready to make any major decisions about my future without you."

"Matt, you can't expect me to plan your future."

"I know I want you to be part of it," Matt insisted.

"How can you be so sure?" Kylie asked. "We really only dated a few weeks when I was in Virginia. We were barely getting to know each other."

Matt linked his fingers with hers. "We were together long enough for me to fall in love with you."

"I was vulnerable then." Kylie shook her head. "I think you fell in love with a scared little girl who needed protection."

"Maybe, but the Lord brought us together again." Matt leaned closer. "I think we owe it to ourselves to find out why."

"It scares me when you're right." Kylie reached up and rubbed her hand along his cheek.

"Is there a night this week I could take you out to dinner or something?" Matt asked, hoping she'd give him another chance.

"I'm free tomorrow night. That is, if you don't have plans with your parents."

"They're leaving in the morning. My game tomorrow should be over by about five." A slow smile spread across his face. "What time can I pick you up?"

"How about seven?"

"I think we should try going to a nice restaurant for a change." Matt stood, pulling her up from her chair. "I'll walk you out to your car."

Kylie nodded, noticing how comfortable her hand felt in his. When she disengaged the car alarm, he opened the door for her. He squeezed her hand and stepped back.

"See you tomorrow," Kylie said before he closed her door.

Matt smiled. "I'm looking forward to it."

CHAPTER 13

Matt was surprised that Jill answered the door when he came to pick Kylie up. The apologetic look on her face had him wondering if Kylie was going to back out of their date.

"Matt, come on in." Jill motioned to the living room where Brooke was watching television. "Kylie is still getting ready. Her practice ran late tonight."

"She's not planning on standing me up then?" Matt asked half seriously.

Brooke clicked off the television. "Not that we would let her if she wanted to, but she has been looking forward to tonight."

"She even bought a new dress," Jill whispered.

Matt leaned closer. "That's a good thing, right?"

"Oh yeah."

Matt grinned, glad to know that Kylie's roommates were on his side. He could see why Kylie had become such close friends with them. They were both so genuine and easygoing, and they shared the sense of humor he was just beginning to appreciate in Kylie.

When Kylie appeared in the living room, he had to catch his breath. Though her hair was still damp, she had taken the time to put on makeup. Her periwinkle dress brought out flecks of blue in her normally gray eyes, and the heels she wore showed off her slender legs.

"Have you been waiting long?" Kylie asked apologetically.

"A few minutes." Matt stood. "It was worth the wait."

Kylie's cheeks flushed as Matt took her arm and escorted her to the door.

"See you later," Matt called out as he guided Kylie out into the night air.

"I'm sorry I was running late," Kylie apologized again as Matt opened the car door for her. "Practice ran over."

Matt closed her door and soon climbed in the driver's seat. "We have plenty of time. Our reservation isn't until seven-thirty."

Kylie glanced down at her watch to see that they still had fifteen minutes to spare. "Were you expecting me to be late?"

"I just don't like to rush." Matt glanced at her as he pulled onto the street. "I guess we're not a secret anymore."

"I think we stopped being a secret when you sent me those muffins," Kylie laughed. "That made me so mad!"

"It was supposed to." Matt grinned. "I haven't been able to figure out your swimming schedule, and I couldn't think of any other way to get you out of your apartment."

"You tried to get me mad so I would go swim?" Kylie's eyes widened.

"Yep," Matt admitted easily.

"Maybe you do know me better than I gave you credit for." Kylie shook her head.

"I'm sure there's still a lot I don't know," Matt told her. "For example, when do you practice?"

"It depends on the day. I always practice from ten to noon." Kylie smoothed her dress over her knees. "Then I usually practice again from three to five, but sometimes I get bumped back to seven to nine at night, depending on what's scheduled."

"When are you usually home?"

"Most of my classes are in the afternoons, so I'm home in the morning before practice and again in the evenings after practice," Kylie told him. "What about you? I imagine that your schedule is getting hectic now that your regular season has started."

"I'm not even sure what my schedule is. We have an afternoon game tomorrow and a double-header the next day. Then we're on the road for three night games." Matt shook his head.

"Sounds busy," Kylie agreed.

Matt parked outside the restaurant and leaned over to open the glove compartment. "I almost forgot." He pulled an envelope out and handed it to Kylie. "I meant to give these to you."

Kylie opened the envelope to see a copy of his game schedule and three season passes. "You didn't have to do this."

"It's purely selfish of me," Matt told her, pausing to get out of the car and open her door. "I like having you at my games. And I wouldn't expect you to come see me alone. Brooke and Jill seemed to enjoy the games they came to."

Kylie tucked the envelope into her purse. "They both love sports."

As they approached the door, Matt took her hands in his, turning her to face him. "Kylie, I don't want you to think I expect you to come to all of my games or anything. I just want you to know that you're the only person that I look for in the stands."

Kylie squeezed his hands. "I'll be there when I can."

Matt nodded and led her inside. As they sat down at the candlelit table, her face softened, and Matt tried to memorize the moment, hoping he could capture it on paper.

As he ordered for both of them, Kylie was struck with how easily the conversation flowed between them, and the tense moments of the past few weeks seemed to fade away.

After dinner, Matt accepted Kylie's invitation to come inside once they reached her apartment. Brooke and Jill were both still home—an unusual occurrence for a Saturday night—watching a movie on television.

When they started to leave Kylie and Matt alone, it was Matt who insisted they hang out with them. Kylie dug out their game of Pictionary as Matt challenged her roommates to a game. He soon found out how accurate Brooke had been when she told him that none of them could draw.

"There's no way we can beat you guys," Brooke said after losing miserably to Matt and Kylie.

"Hey, you were the one who bought this game." Kylie grinned.

"Tell you what. The winners will buy ice cream," Matt offered, standing up.

"Oh, we're fine," Jill insisted, expecting Kylie and Matt to leave them behind.

Matt offered his hand to Kylie to help her up and then offered a hand to each of her roommates. "Come on." He nodded toward the door. "I'll be the envy of every guy in the place."

"I get shotgun," Kylie said as she opened the door and waited for Brooke and Jill.

Matt drove to the ice cream parlor near the college, finding it crowded with students. He just grinned when several guys turned to watch them all walk in. And his jaw dropped when he heard Jill and Brooke order. He already knew that Kylie could have a decent appetite, but to watch three slender, beautiful women order mega-calorie desserts was mind-boggling.

"I'll get us a table," Brooke told him. "You bring the ice cream."

"Don't forget the spoons," Jill added, joining Brooke at a now-vacated table.

"Do they always eat like this?" Matt asked, turning to Kylie.

Kylie nodded. "That's why they both work out every day."

"I'm surprised neither of them had dates tonight," Matt commented.

"They double-date a lot." Kylie glanced over at her roommates, who were already chatting with the guys at the next table. "Brooke's still hung up on a missionary she sent off more than a year ago."

"What about Jill?"

"She just hasn't found anyone who appreciates her mind as well as her looks." Kylie shrugged. "Most people see what she looks like and don't bother to find out that she's smart too."

After their order arrived, Matt set the tray down on the table and watched the food disappear. He had just started on his hot fudge sundae when someone tapped his shoulder.

"Hey, aren't you Matt Whitmore?" The guy standing behind Matt appeared to be about Kylie's age.

Matt nodded, his mouth full of hot fudge.

"I saw you play last night." The young man rocked back on the heels of his feet. "You hit that sacrifice fly in the ninth. That was awesome."

"Thanks."

"Hey, can I get your autograph?"

Matt took the paper that had been shoved in front of him and signed. "Here you go."

"This is great. Man, my roommates aren't going to believe this." His gaze swept over the girls at the table. Shaking his head, he walked away muttering, "I should have been a ball player."

Kylie stifled a giggle; Jill bit her lip, successfully keeping her composure; and Brooke just shook her head as she shoveled another bite of ice cream into her mouth.

"I didn't think guys got that excited over minor leaguers." Matt shook his head.

Brooke just patted his arm. "Honey, you're just getting started."

* * *

Kylie shifted in her seat, trying to stay focused on what her sociology teacher was saying. She listened to some of her classmates discuss the function of love and marriage in society, knowing that they lacked so much essential knowledge simply by not having the gospel in their lives. Her mind wandered to Matt's parents. Unwittingly, they had set the standard of marriage she wanted for herself—a partnership based on love and trust, with a strong reliance on the Lord for guidance. Why would anyone want to settle for less?

As her mind wandered, Kylie thought of Matt. She wasn't sure what to think of her new relationship with him. In the past two weeks since they had started dating again, he had taken her out six times, and it wasn't until their fourth date that he had even kissed her goodnight. Oddly enough, she hadn't expected him to.

She couldn't pinpoint when she had started keeping track of his schedule, or when he had started informing her of his travel plans for his away trips. She wasn't even sure how they managed to find time to spend together between her practice schedule and his crazy schedule of practices, games, and the frequent travel that kept him away from home as often as not.

Brooke and Jill had come with her to several of his home games, often going out with Matt and Kylie afterward. Initially they had expected Matt to take Kylie home after his games, but they soon realized that Matt enjoyed having them along too.

As Matt became a constant presence in their apartment, Kylie realized just how much fun he was to be around. Their phone conversations lengthened and their friendship deepened, and Kylie found herself falling in love with him all over again. Kylie still looked forward to those moments they spent alone, but the fact that he tried to see her when others were around made her appreciate his respect for her. Though she knew she was welcome at his apartment, they were both uncomfortable when they were there alone. It just didn't feel right since he didn't have any roommates. Her respect for him grew when she came home one day and found him sincerely trying to console Brooke, who was in tears and holding a letter in her trembling hands.

"What's wrong?" Kylie dropped her swim bag on the floor and kicked the door closed behind her.

Matt kept his arm around Brooke's shoulders as Brooke blotted her eyes with a tissue.

Brooke just shook her head, unable to speak.

"She got a letter from her missionary," Matt said softly.

"It doesn't look like it was good news." Kylie sat down on the other side of Brooke. "What did it say?"

"His parents are moving next month." Brooke sniffled. "To Alaska."

"What?" Kylie looked from Brooke to Matt.

"I may never see him again." Brooke sniffed again.

"If it's meant to be, you'll find a way," Kylie insisted.

Brooke looked up, her eyes still misty. "That's what Matt said."

Kylie just smiled.

Brooke stood, looking from Matt to Kylie. "Thanks."

They watched her make her way down the hall, hearing her bedroom door shut a moment later.

"How much do you want to bet that they're married within six months of his return?" Matt asked, nodding toward the hall.

Kylie sighed. "I hope everything works out."

"It will," Matt said softly, moving closer to her on the couch. "It has for us, hasn't it?"

"Yeah, it has." Kylie smiled.

CHAPTER 14

Jill sighed wistfully as she smelled the pink carnations on the kitchen table. She didn't have to ask to know that they were for Kylie. Flowers frequently showed up when Matt left on a road trip, as did silly postcards originating from Matt's various stops along the way. It wasn't that she hadn't received flowers before. She had. In fact, she figured she had probably already received more than her share. But never from someone who truly mattered to her.

She kicked off the ridiculously high heels she had worn on her date and sat down in a chair to rub her feet. Her date of the evening had been pleasant enough. He said the right things, opened the doors for her, and was as boring as a ninety-year-old history professor.

Just once, Jill wished for a man who would add a little excitement to her life. She wanted someone who could make her heart beat faster just by walking into the room, someone she could laugh with, someone who would look at her the way Matt looked at Kylie.

When the doorbell rang, Jill stood, leaving her shoes behind. She opened the door in her stocking feet and looked up into the most incredible brown eyes she had ever seen.

She took a quick breath as the man's smile softened his face. His dark hair was cut military short, and his chiseled features just escaped being handsome.

Though it took some effort, Jill managed to swallow. She thought she wanted someone who would make her heart beat faster. Now that her heart was pounding in her chest, she wasn't so sure she liked the sensation, or the unease of having her thoughts transformed into reality in an instant.

"Wow." He exhaled slowly. "Kylie didn't tell me her roommate was such a knockout."

Jill stiffened, her back straightening as she kept her eyes on his. Her voice was almost regal as she spoke. "And you would be . . ."

"Doug Valdez." Doug offered his hand to Jill, who shook it reluctantly. "Kylie's cousin."

"Cousin?" Jill looked at him suspiciously, then, realizing her hand was still in his, she pulled back. "She didn't mention anything . . ."

"I thought I'd surprise her," Doug told her. "I'll be in town for most of the week."

"I'm afraid she isn't here," Jill said. Manners dictated that she let him in, but she wasn't entirely sure she trusted this man standing on her doorstep.

"Let me guess." Doug stepped forward, keeping his eyes on hers. "She's at the pool training for the Olympics."

Jill's stance relaxed slightly.

"Do I pass the test?" Doug grinned.

Stepping back from the door, Jill motioned him inside. "I'm sorry. You can't be too careful these days."

"You're telling me." Doug took a seat on the couch, waiting for Jill to sit across from him. "How long ago did she leave?"

Jill glanced down at her watch. "She should be back pretty soon."

"I guess we'll just have to get to know each other while we wait." Doug leaned forward, resting his elbows on his knees. "Tell me about yourself."

* * *

Jill's laughter rang out as Kylie opened the front door. She had already closed the door behind her when she looked up and saw him.

"What did I do to deserve this?" Kylie's voice was laced with a sarcasm that almost hid her concern at seeing Doug sitting in her living room.

Doug leaped up and pulled Kylie into a bear hug. "Hey, cuz."

"Isn't it customary to call before you just drop in on someone?"

"I was in the neighborhood."

"That's what you always say." Kylie pushed her damp hair behind her ears and shook her head. "I see you met Jill."

Doug nodded. "Yeah. I just convinced her to go to dinner with me tomorrow night."

Kylie's mouth fell open before she could stop it. "You're hitting on my roommate?"

"Can you blame me?" Doug motioned to Jill, who was now standing behind them. "How often do you find someone that looks like this and has a brain too?"

Now Jill's jaw dropped.

"What do you say we all go catch a late movie?" Doug suggested.

Jill looked at Kylie for approval and then agreed. "That sounds like fun. I just need to go change."

Jill disappeared down the hall, leaving them alone.

"What are you doing here?" Kylie asked in a hushed voice.

Doug patted her shoulder. "Don't worry. This is just a routine check on your cover. Besides, I was going to be picking you up next week anyway."

Kylie sighed. "I'm going to have to testify again?"

"Yeah. This guy refuses to plea-bargain." Doug thought of the extra security he had arranged for her and quickly changed the subject, motioning to the shorts she wore. "You might want to change. It looks like it's going to rain."

"I'll be back in a minute." Kylie hauled her duffel bag into her bedroom and returned a few minutes later wearing jeans and a T-shirt. She just prayed that Jill wouldn't mention Matt to her "cousin."

"Are you ready?" Jill asked, picking up her purse.

Kylie nodded, walking through the door Doug held open for them. She insisted Jill sit in the front of the car with Doug, wondering how to tell her that her cousin wasn't Mormon. She didn't have to wait long for the subject to come up. As they were discussing which movie to see, Doug expressed his preference for an action movie that was rated R.

"Doug, Jill's Mormon too. We don't watch R-rated movies, remember?"

"Sorry. I'm not up on all the rules of that religion of yours." Doug shrugged casually. "I'll let you two pick."

They settled on a romantic comedy with an acceptable PG rating. Even though Doug tried hard not to like it, he was laughing the hardest of the three of them before it was over.

"Are you going to try to tell us that it was a 'chick flick' now?" Kylie asked, not even flinching when Doug slung his arm companionably around her shoulder.

"I hate it when you make me admit I'm wrong."

"I would think you would be used to it by now." Kylie grinned. "It happens so often."

"Ouch." Doug placed his hand over his heart.

"Are you two sure you're not brother and sister?" Jill asked as she watched the constant teasing going on between them.

Doug just laughed.

Kylie slid into the backseat of the car, thinking back to the first time she had dealt with Doug. He had pretended to be her boyfriend to keep Matt from being part of her life. He had been so annoying at the time, and yet it had been Doug who had arranged for her to see Matt one last time before she was moved here to Texas.

He had taken over as her agent-in-charge when her previous agent had taken an early retirement. Part of his duties during the past year had been to escort her to the numerous hearings and trials to help convict the members of the smuggling organization that was responsible for Chase's murder.

After spending so much time together, they had practically become family. Constant teasing and bickering came naturally to them, and no one had questioned whether or not they were related since he had begun to claim Kylie as his "cousin" a year before.

Doug saw them to their door but didn't come in, bidding them good-bye on the doorstep.

As soon as they were inside, Kylie collapsed on the couch.

"Kylie, you are so lucky." Jill just shook her head, sitting down next to her.

"What do you mean?"

"First you end up with Matt, an up-and-coming baseball player, not to mention a great guy." Jill nodded at the door. "And you have a cousin who obviously adores you."

"Just do me a favor and don't mention to Doug that I'm dating anyone." Kylie took a deep breath, choosing her words carefully. "He gets really overprotective, and I don't need that right now."

"What if he asks?" Jill asked. Lying wasn't in her nature, but she would never want to betray a confidence either.

"Just say something like, 'You know how Kylie is,' and he'll assume I'm not dating." As she looked at Jill, a grin crossed her face. "You like him, don't you?"

Jill leaned her head back and looked up at the ceiling. "I was just thinking how boring all of the guys are that I date, and how none of them even acknowledges that I can think on my own. Then Doug shows up at the door with that wicked grin of his."

"He is pretty good-looking."

"Now that's an understatement."

Kylie laughed.

"And in less than half an hour, he's complimenting me on having a brain." Jill picked up the throw pillow behind her, hugging it to her chest.

"And a great body."

"He didn't exactly phrase it like that."

"No, but he was thinking it," Kylie teased. She didn't even flinch when Jill threw the pillow right at her face.

"I can't believe you said that!" Jill tried to look annoyed and then giggled.

Kylie tossed the pillow back at her. "Does it bother you that he isn't Mormon?"

"I was kind of surprised when it came up," Jill admitted. "I just assumed that he was since he's related to you."

"He doesn't know much about the Church," Kylie told her. "If he hangs around you long enough, he might learn something."

"You never know."

* * *

Kylie lay back on her bed, the cordless phone cradled against her ear as she listened to Matt describe his last game. She was finally beginning to understand the various statistics and baseball terminology he used so casually. Just weeks before, most of it had been foreign to her. She tried not to think about how their relationship had settled into a routine she now depended on. Matt's schedule was tacked to her bulletin board, and she had already grown accustomed to his nightly phone calls.

She grabbed the stuffed dolphin off the pillow and tossed it in the air above her, catching it before it dropped on her. Her mind turned to the day she had gotten the little dolphin, the day that Chase had been killed. The ache that his loss caused had settled deep within her, alongside the pang of loneliness she sometimes suffered when she thought of her father. The summer she lost them both still seemed surreal at times, as though it had all been a dream. Yet, she was still Christal in her dreams.

The stuffed animal was the only thing she owned that had survived all three of her identities. Now, she marveled that her relationship with Matt had survived their separation over the past year. When she had first met him, Kylie remembered thinking that he was the kind of person who could be trusted, someone with whom she wished she could share confidences. In fact, while she had initially been forced to hide her true identity from him, she had worried that he so clearly expected loyalty and honesty from those close to him.

After she was forced to assume another identity for a time, he had promised to wait for her as though she had been leaving on a mission or going away to college. They had both tried not to admit that she was leaving to hide once again to protect her life. As Matt continued to relay some of the highlights of the game that night, Kylie realized that they still avoided the topic of Chris Rush and the fact that she was still in hiding.

As their conversation became more personal, Kylie toyed with the idea of telling Matt about Doug coming to town but ultimately decided against it. She knew he was nervous about his upcoming games against the number-one team in his division, and it didn't seem necessary to give him one more thing to worry about. The timing of his road trip perfectly coincided with the next trial date. Matt would get home the day after she would.

Since his last two games on the road were night games, he wasn't even likely to be able to call her and not find her home. Kylie tossed the dolphin up in the air again, snagging its tail in midair. She ignored the knock on her door, glancing over only when the door opened.

"I need the phone," Brooke insisted.

Kylie just nodded, then waited until Matt finished his sentence before interrupting. "I'm going to have to go. Brooke's making noise about needing the phone."

"I'll call you tomorrow." Matt lowered his voice before adding, "I love you."

Kylie caught her breath. He hadn't told her that for weeks—not since they had first gone out after finding each other again. And hearing the words, she knew her feelings for him had only gotten stronger. "I love you too."

"You know, I could get used to hearing you say that."

"I guess I'll have to get used to saying it." Kylie smiled, cuddling the little dolphin to her chest.

"Talk to you tomorrow."

After hanging up, Kylie rolled herself off the bed, tossing the stuffed animal back onto the pillow. She found Brooke to tell her she could use the phone. Brooke was just finishing on the phone when Jill and Doug got home from their date.

Jill was laughing, Doug was grinning like a fool, and Kylie just stared, wondering how two people she knew so well could change before her eyes. Before Brooke and Kylie could clear the room, Doug took Jill's hand in his.

"I'll see you tomorrow then." Doug squeezed Jill's hand. He winked at Kylie before backing out the door. "Stay out of trouble."

Kylie just shook her head when Jill watched Doug leave and then leaned against the door with a sigh.

Brooke hung up the phone and walked over to Jill, putting a hand on her forehead. "Oh, yeah. She's got it bad."

Jill pushed her hand away, shaking her head. "Stop it."

"He's so annoying," Kylie confided in Brooke. "I don't how she can stand to be around him."

"You're terrible." Jill suppressed a grin. "Talking about your own cousin like that."

"My nonmember cousin," Kylie pointed out.

"I gave him a Book of Mormon."

"What?" Kylie put a hand out and steadied herself against the wall in mock surprise.

"Somebody had to." Jill just shrugged. "I'm going to bed."

Kylie just watched her go and then shook her head. "She never ceases to amaze me."

CHAPTER 15

Never in a million years would Kylie have expected to see Doug at an LDS fireside—especially one on a Saturday night. Of course, he had come with Jill, not her, which made the whole scene that much more surreal.

Kylie considered how strange it was to see him here. Doug had been her protector for more than a year, but these two areas of her life had always been separate before.

She watched Doug sitting down with Jill in the chapel, and Caitlin walked up behind her. "Hi, Kylie. Where's Matt tonight?"

Kylie was surprised, realizing that the rumor mill was working faster than she had thought. She glanced nervously at Doug, grateful he was out of hearing distance. "He's still on a road trip."

"Oh, that's right. He mentioned he would miss our next family home evening." Caitlin chose a seat and slid into one of the pews as Brooke approached.

"Hi, Caitlin." Brooke followed her into the pew. "Can we sit with you?"

"Sure." Caitlin nodded toward Jill. "Who's that with Jill?"

"Kylie's cousin," Brooke told her as the meeting began.

Kylie leaned back in her seat, deciding that this was as good a place as any to pray for help in making it through the night.

* * *

Doug observed the stream of people coming through the chapel doors for the fireside. Most of the attendees seemed to be in their twenties. Several people stopped by to greet Jill, and Doug found himself introduced to at least thirty people before the fireside began.

He could easily remember the last time he had attended church. Each Christmas and Easter, his parents insisted they go to Mass. Rarely did any of his family members attend church at other times during the year, and if they did, it was likely because of a birth or a death in the family. Occasionally, he came across people like Jill who attended church every week and then some, but never before had anyone invited him along. He still wasn't sure how she had convinced him to join her tonight.

When the organist began to play, Doug glanced around, waiting for everyone to stand up. When they all remained in their seats during the hymn, he shrugged and remained seated. As the prayer was offered, he glanced down at the pew in front of him, realizing for the first time that there was nothing there to kneel on. Again, everyone remained seated.

The man who stood up to speak was small in stature, standing only about five-foot-eight. His hair was snowy white against his weathered, olive complexion, and he spoke with a slight European accent. His voice carried through the chapel, and he spoke calmly and clearly, yet his account brought chills to everyone within earshot. He told of his childhood during World War II and the many miracles that had occurred to help him and many of his family members survive.

As the man spoke of his first introduction to the gospel, Doug felt goose bumps rise on his arms. He rubbed a hand absently over one arm as though to warm it, and then cautiously slid his hand into Jill's, linking their fingers.

He stared down at their joined hands, surprised that she didn't resist or seem uncomfortable. After their first date, Doug had been more than a little taken aback when Jill had merely opted for a friendly hug good night, blocking any attempt he would have made to kiss her. They had been out two other times since that night, each with similar endings. Now, her hand was warm in his and it felt as though it belonged there. He rubbed his thumb over the smooth skin on the back of her hand. The thought that this was a woman his parents would approve of left him almost as surprised as his parents would have been to find him sitting in an LDS church. Of course, he could already hear the ribbing he would take from his sister if he were to tell her he was dating an elementary schoolteacher.

His plan to slip away with Jill as soon as the fireside ended vanished when he found himself chatting with a group of her friends. It was nearly ten o'clock before he and Jill settled into a booth at the local diner, sharing a hot fudge sundae.

"Do you go to these fireside things often?" Doug asked eventually.

"We have a fireside every couple of months or so." Jill swirled her spoon in her ice cream. "What did you think of tonight's speaker?"

Doug lifted a shoulder in response. How could he answer her? If he admitted that he was impressed, she might make more out of it than it was, but lying to her was something that he found he couldn't do.

Jill spooned up another bite, savoring the taste of hot fudge. "You and Kylie are leaving tomorrow morning?"

"Yeah." Doug nodded, grateful that she had changed the subject. "We'll only be gone a few days."

The waitress appeared with the check before Jill could respond, and Doug pulled out a few bills as Jill slid out of the booth. As they left the restaurant, he took her hand, grateful to have the privilege. Never before had he dated a girl whom he had enjoyed being with so much. He certainly couldn't remember the last time he had gone on a date with someone without a kiss good night.

When they arrived back at Jill's apartment, Doug skirted the front of his car and opened her door for her. He offered his hand to help her out, pleased that she took it and didn't try to pull away. His mouth was dry as he stared down at her, realizing that she was absolute perfection in every way. His first impression that she was smart and beautiful had been only partially correct. As they had continued to spend time together, Doug had found that her beauty went much deeper.

As they approached her doorstep, Doug managed to ask, "Would you mind terribly if I were to kiss you good night?"

Jill kept her eyes on his, unable to find her voice. She had managed to keep Doug at arm's length during their first few dates, but somehow tonight she had found herself weakening. Never before had she considered seriously dating a nonmember, at least not since she had returned from her mission. Now, she felt trapped by her growing feelings for him, and she couldn't bring herself to pull back.

She had wondered what it would be like to kiss him. In fact, at the end of each date, she felt like she had won a small victory each time she escaped inside with no more than a hug. She knew now that each date had edged her closer to this moment.

When she didn't answer his question, Doug stepped closer and ran his hands down her arms, linking both hands with hers. He ran his thumb over one wrist, finding to his pleasure that her pulse was quickening. Slowly, he lowered his lips to hers. He brushed them softly once, then twice. Jill's eyes fluttered closed as his hand released hers, and he lifted his hand to cup the back of her neck.

It cost him to draw back, to remember who and what she was. Never before had a woman changed any aspect of his life. He had always enjoyed women's company and spending time with them. But when the evening was over, he had always before been content to return to his life. As he looked down into Jill's eyes, he wasn't sure he could walk away from her and remain the same.

* * *

"You really believe that people can be married forever, even after they die?" Doug sat across from Kylie as they ate dinner in her hotel suite. Two U.S. Marshals had already taken their positions outside the door.

Kylie nodded, savoring the bite of cheesecake she had just put in her mouth.

"And you really think this Joseph Smith guy wrote your Book of Mormon?"

"Translated," Kylie said, her fork slicing through her dessert. "Joseph Smith translated the Book of Mormon."

"You and Jill talk like you know that for sure." Doug pushed the food around his plate, surprised his appetite had diminished.

"We do." Kylie stood and disappeared into the bedroom, returning a moment later with her triple combination. She flipped through the Book of Mormon until she found the passage she was looking for. "If you want to know what we know, just do what the book says."

Doug took the book from her, scanning the scripture that was already marked—Moroni 10:4. "Ask God, the Eternal Father, in the name of Christ, if these things are not true."

Kylie just watched as he read and reread the scripture to himself.

"You expect me to ask God to tell me that this book is true?" Doug's eyes widened. "You're kidding, right?"

Shaking her head, Kylie picked up her fork. "You do what that scripture says, and you'll know that this book is true, just like I do." She indulged in another bite of dessert, watching him consider her words. Then she added, "Notice it says in there you have to 'ask with a sincere heart, with real intent, having faith in Christ.'"

Doug looked down at the scripture and then back at her. "What, did you memorize this or something?"

Kylie pushed her plate back and looked him in the eye. Warmth spread through her as she felt the Spirit. "I know this book is true, just like I know that God lives. I know that Jesus Christ died for us so that all of us can live again with our Heavenly Father. And I know that when a couple gets married in the temple, they are married for eternity, not just until 'death do you part.'"

Doug sat silently for a moment before finally standing. "I'd better get going. Try to get some sleep."

Kylie glanced down at her Book of Mormon still sitting on the table. She lifted it up and asked, "Do you want to borrow this?"

"I've got my own."

* * *

Doug passed Kylie off to another agent the next day, and after spending several hours riding in a car, she was passed off again to the U.S. Marshals who would escort and protect her through the current trial.

The trial was rigorous and emotionally draining. Kylie had been cross-examined often enough to know that she would go back to her hotel room in tears. Every time she testified, she had to relive Chase's last night alive. And every time, she wondered by what miracle her life had been spared. Still, as she was ushered into the courthouse each day with her armed escort, she knew that her life was not yet her own.

Her head pounded as she settled back on the couch in her suite, hoping to forget the threats the defendant had shouted at her just hours before. The knock on the door had her wincing in pain as she pressed her fingers to her temples.

Rising slowly, she crossed the room and opened the door. Tara Baldino, one of the female marshals, passed through the doorway with a nod to the two men standing outside in the hall. She had been assigned to Kylie before, one of the youngest of the marshals to be trusted with her protection.

"The judge has approved a 24-hour continuance." Baldino surveyed the room, her expression unreadable when her gaze came back to Kylie. "We may have to delay your return trip."

"Great," Kylie muttered, dropping onto the couch. "When will I know?"

"Day after tomorrow." Marshal Baldino crossed the room, pulling back the curtains far enough to glance out the window at the drizzling rain. Turning, she looked at Kylie, compassion showing in her eyes. "Don't let them get to you. We'll get you back home before you know it."

Kylie nodded, wishing she had told Matt that she was testifying again. Of course, she could only hope he would figure it out if he beat her back home.

CHAPTER 16

Matt stood on Kylie's doorstep, not quite sure how he had gotten there. He had tried calling right after walking in the door from his road trip, but after five minutes of getting a busy signal, he had jumped into his car and driven to her apartment without a second thought.

"Matt!" Jill opened the door wide and motioned him inside. "When did you get back?"

"Just a little while ago." Matt glanced around the apartment, noticing Brooke with the phone to her ear. "Is Kylie here?"

"No, actually . . ." Jill began.

"Let me guess." Matt shook his head. "She's at the pool."

"Um, no." Jill glanced over to Brooke, who deliberately stayed on the phone. "She's out of town."

"Where?" Matt felt a prickle of panic sneak up his spine.

"She went to visit her cousin."

"Her cousin?"

"Yeah. Doug dropped in right after you left town. Then Kylie went home with him for some family thing."

Matt's eyes widened as a surge of jealousy surfaced. "Doug Valdez?"

Jill nodded. "Have you met him?"

"She's mentioned him before." Matt tried to calm his nerves as he rationalized Kylie's absence. She must have had to testify again. "Does she visit her family very often?"

"This is the first time in a while, but last summer she was gone all the time. She goes in spurts."

Matt nodded, feeling a little better. "Do you know when she's supposed to get back?"

"Sometime today." Jill shrugged, wringing her hands together. "I'm surprised she's not home by now."

"Let her know I stopped by," Matt said before slipping back out the door.

Jill watched him go, fighting back her concern. She hadn't told Matt that Kylie had expected to get home that morning and was already almost twelve hours late. Her concern was made worse by the fact that Kylie's cell phone was turned off.

Brooke hung up the phone and picked it up to make another call. Before she could finish dialing, Jill snatched the phone out of her hand.

"Hey, I need that!" Brooke reached for the phone.

"What if Kylie is trying to call us and you're on the phone?" Jill demanded. "They might have broken down somewhere."

"I'm sure they're both fine," Brooke insisted, knowing that Jill was just as worried about Doug as she was about Kylie. "They probably just decided to stay another day and didn't think to call us."

"Maybe, but that isn't like Kylie not to call," Jill fretted.

"Don't worry. We'll hear from them soon."

Another day passed. The next night, Jill and Brooke were both sitting on the couch staring at the phone when it rang. Brooke was the first to pounce on it, snatching it up with an eager "Hello?"

Standing right behind her, Jill strained to hear who was on the line. Brooke stepped away, turning to Jill. "It's Matt."

"Has he heard from them?" Jill asked eagerly.

Brooke held a hand up to wave off her roommate, unable to hold two conversations at once.

"She isn't home yet, Matt," Brooke said, shaking her head as she heard Matt's anxiety level rise to meet her own. "She was supposed to get back yesterday morning. Jill even tried calling Doug's house, but all she got was his voice mail."

Dropping back down on the couch with the phone still cradled between her shoulder and ear, Brooke fought to keep her voice steady. "Yeah, Matt. We'll call you as soon as we hear something."

Jill's eyes were already wet with tears by the time Brooke hung up. "Where could she be?"

"I don't know, Jill." Brooke shook her head. "I just don't know."

* * *

Kylie stepped down from the witness stand, emotionally and physically exhausted. The tears that had threatened to spill over during her testimony glistened in her eyes, and she attempted once again to blink them away as she was escorted from the courtroom. She didn't look at the defendant against whom she had just testified.

Experience had taught her that the men sitting on the defendant's side of the courtroom were capable of looking like normal, everyday people. She had learned to concentrate only on the truth. How it applied to the defendant would be up to the panel of jurors.

Two U.S. Marshals flanked her as she exited the courtroom, and Kylie was surprised when one of them took her by the arm and turned her away from the main entrance. Confused, she looked up at him to see the sense of urgency in his eyes. Her heartbeat quickened as she lengthened her stride to keep up with the two men escorting her.

"What's wrong?" Kylie managed as one of the agents pushed open the stairwell door.

"We'll explain later." He held one finger up to his lips, signaling her to keep quiet.

Obediently, Kylie followed him to an exit at the back of the building. Just outside the door, Marshal Baldino was waiting for them with the car. She waited a moment, then signaled that it was clear. Quickly Kylie was pulled out into the bright sunlight toward the black sedan. They were nearly to the car when the first bullet whizzed by, striking the rear tire. Kylie didn't hear the sound of the sniper's rifle from the rooftop across the street, but her protectors reacted instinctively, pushing her to the ground.

A scream pierced the air. Kylie didn't recognize the sound as coming from her, nor did she feel the hand keeping her head down as she was lifted from the ground and shoved into the waiting car. A bullet lodged in the windshield, and Kylie drew her hands up over her head when she heard the bulletproof glass crack. Outside, voices shouted. A burst of gunfire was followed by another single shot, this one ringing off the body of the car. Kylie would learn later that the armor of the car had kept the bullet from penetrating the back door behind which she lay.

This can't be happening, Kylie thought to herself. Her life wasn't supposed to end this way. She had dreams, plans for her life. She thought of Matt and the way he sometimes spoke about marriage. *I'm supposed to marry him someday,* Kylie thought now, surprised at how strongly she felt it to be true. Another burst of gunfire rang out, and Kylie realized that someday might not ever come.

She heard a marshal jump into the driver's seat and rev the engine to life. Metal and rubber squealed against the pavement as the car raced away from the courthouse. Kylie squeezed her eyes closed and concentrated on the simple task of breathing.

* * *

A second-grade history book lay on Jill's lap, and she was trying diligently to plan her lesson for the next day. She already had begun the section on Johnny Appleseed three times and was currently contemplating starting on her fourth. Why couldn't she concentrate?

Sure, she was worried about Kylie. She could even admit that she was worried about Doug. Yet until this week, she had always been able to push problems aside to finish the work at hand. She thought back to her junior year in college. With two days of final exams remaining, her beloved grandfather had passed away. She had certainly grieved, but she had forced herself to schedule that grief between studying and exams. Though difficult, she had learned to harness her emotions and concern for her family until she could afford the luxury to let it all out. She had always known that some things had to be done whether life was going well or not.

Now, staring down at the elementary textbook, she knew that her concern was not the only thing keeping her up at night. She continued to remind herself that if anything bad had happened, surely someone would have notified them by now. Matt and Brooke had both offered similar assurances.

As each day wore on, however, her feelings for Doug left her unsure and too emotionally crippled to function normally. Her students were blessedly too naive and innocent to notice anything unusual about their teacher. Some of her coworkers, though, had begun to express concern upon seeing the swollen eyes that makeup couldn't quite hide.

"I never should have let him kiss me," Jill muttered to herself. She closed her eyes, squeezing them tight to ward off another crying bout. It hadn't been *just a kiss,* even though Jill tried to categorize it as just that. Somehow, he had gotten to her in a way no one else had.

I really do care for him, Jill realized suddenly. The admission caused her slight discomfort as she also admitted that he didn't share her innermost religious beliefs.

The tears she had been holding back fell freely now. Never had she thought that she could be so affected by someone after such a short amount of time. As a young teenager, she had promised herself to marry in the temple. She thought of the Book of Mormon she had given Doug and the questions he had asked. After their first date, she had spent much of her time on her knees, asking for guidance from her Heavenly Father. Repeatedly she had asked if she should stop dating Doug, but each time she thought of doing so, she felt an uncomfortable tightness in her chest. She knew that Doug had felt the Spirit at the fireside, yet she sensed he was afraid to speak of his feelings.

Her thoughts were interrupted by the telephone. She pounced on it only to find Matt on the other end. Their conversation was a repeat of those held earlier in the week. No, they had not heard from her and yes, they would continue to pray. As tears welled in her eyes, Jill knew that from this point on, her prayers would take a whole new direction.

* * *

Matt slammed the phone down, staring at it in disbelief. Maybe there was a logical explanation as to why no one had heard from her, but Matt had seen how protective custody worked before. One minute the woman he loved was part of his life, and then suddenly she just vanished as if she had never been there at all.

During the first three days of her prolonged absence, Matt had made up excuses as to why Kylie had not yet returned. A trial had been delayed. They missed a flight. A car broke down. But after nearly a week of waiting by the phone every spare moment, Matt convinced himself that she had been relocated again.

Glancing up at the sketch on the wall, he paced through his apartment as anger replaced frustration. He wasn't going to lose her again. He just wasn't. Doug Valdez had another thought coming if he thought he could just pluck Kylie out of Texas and ship her off to a new identity without a word.

Matt pushed aside his guilt, knowing that he was the most likely reason the FBI would decide to relocate Kylie without any warning. Each time he talked to her roommates, he bit his tongue to keep from telling them everything. He had no doubt that they could be trusted, but he knew that confiding in them would betray Kylie's trust in him.

Jill and Brooke were becoming more frantic, and only a recording on Doug's voice mail—a mention of him leaving town suddenly for a family emergency—had given them any peace of mind. They were hoping Kylie had simply accompanied him wherever he had needed to go. Certainly, Doug would have called if anything had happened to Kylie. Matt continued to assure them of that fact, though he wasn't sure he believed it himself. At least Jill and Brooke were buying it for the time being.

Falling back onto his sofa, Matt dropped his head in his hands. He couldn't keep going on like this, but he didn't know what else he could do. He had loved her when they first knew each other. He both loved and needed her now.

Over the past several weeks, he had blocked out the memories of the difficulty and frustration of being completely cut off both physically and emotionally from Kylie. Now that they were together again, he didn't think he could endure another such separation. As he thought of their current situation, he realized that the emotional ties were the ones he most needed to preserve. His schedule was so demanding that he and Kylie spoke on the phone far more often than they saw one another. He depended on her encouragement and support, and he was beginning to believe that she had come to need him in the same way.

Surely there had to be a way to protect what they had. Though his prayers had been filled with questions and pleas, answers were evading him. There had to be something he could do, some comfort he could find.

As he leaned back, a magazine caught his eye. He reached for the *Ensign* and examined its cover. He looked past the family on the cover to the gleaming white building behind them. What was he waiting for? He loved Kylie. She loved him. They had skirted around the idea of getting married after Chris Rush's trial. Why wait? Even if Doug had to separate them for a time, at least they would be able to insist on some communication—phone calls, letters, something.

He dropped the magazine back onto the table and snatched up his keys. It was about time he took control of his destiny, and part of that destiny was to make sure Kylie would be with him forever. Matt grabbed his jacket and stormed out of the house, a plan already forming in his mind.

CHAPTER 17

Kylie dozed as they drove from one nameless town to another. How long they had been in the car she wasn't sure. She only knew that this must be the last leg of her journey since Doug was at the wheel instead of one of the many other agents she had traveled with during the past week.

She still wasn't sure how the incident outside of the courtroom had been resolved. She doubted Doug would give her the details even if she asked, which she wasn't going to do. Talking about it made it real. Pretending that the attempt on her life was just a horrible nightmare was easier somehow. She hadn't even found any comfort in the news that the verdict of the trial had been the same as the others. Guilty.

She stirred, glancing up as they passed a convoy of tractor trailers on the freeway. "Where are we?"

"It won't be long now," Doug answered simply.

The dull ache behind her eyes began to throb as she shielded them from the headlights of oncoming traffic.

Doug took out a bottle of pills and handed her two. "Take these. They'll take care of that headache."

Nodding, she popped them into her mouth, washing the pills down with her bottled water, which had long since gone warm. Settling back, she closed her eyes, dozing as they passed through the night.

* * *

Matt fingered the small velvet box in his jacket pocket. With a deep breath and a prayer in his heart, he knocked on Kylie's door. It was still shy of eight o'clock in the morning, but he was afraid if he waited to come by until after his morning practice, he might miss Jill and Brooke. If luck was with him, Kylie's roommates could lead him to the next step in his plan.

Brooke yanked the door open, her face showing obvious disappointment when she saw Matt on the doorstep. "You haven't heard from her either?"

Matt just shook his head, following her inside. "I was hoping I could get Doug's phone number from you."

"Why?" Brooke asked, obviously suffering from lack of sleep. "We've already left a dozen messages for him."

"I just figured it wouldn't hurt for both of us to try," Matt told her, hoping she would cooperate.

Brooke shrugged her shoulders. "Can't hurt, I guess." She motioned to the couch. "Go ahead and sit down. I'll have to get it from Jill."

Matt nodded, sitting on the edge of the couch, unable to relax.

When Brooke re-entered the room, Jill was right behind her.

"Hi, Matt." Jill held out a piece of paper with Doug's number on it. "Maybe you'll have better luck than we've had."

"We can only hope."

* * *

The pressure behind her eyes threatened to explode as the light streamed in through the windows. Hoping to find the comfort of darkness, she rolled over without any success. Familiar voices drifted toward her. She struggled to fight her way from sleep into consciousness.

Eyes squinted, she took in the room. Her room. She was home, but she didn't remember how she had gotten there. Shaking her head, she remembered driving with Doug for what seemed like days.

Rolling out of bed, Kylie realized she was still wearing the sweats she had traveled in. She stumbled her first few steps but finally managed to cross the room and open her door. Once she got some food into her stomach, she would be able to think more clearly.

Slowly, she made her way down the hall as the voices drifted toward her. She stepped out into the living room to find three pairs of eyes staring at her.

"Kylie!" all three of them shouted at once.

She winced in pain and made an effort to press her hands to her head, and Matt strode over to her and put his arms around her to help her stand.

"We didn't know you were back." Jill felt the tears threatening. "We've been worried sick about you."

"Where have you been? Why didn't you tell us you were home?" Brooke demanded. "Why didn't you call?"

Kylie looked from her roommates to Matt. He just stood there. His eyes met hers, intense and probing, but when he spoke it was to her roommates. "Do you have any muffins? Kylie has to be starving."

Brooke and Jill looked at each other in shock.

"You don't hear from her for over a week, and you want to know if we have muffins?" Brooke asked incredulously.

"She's obviously had a hard week." Matt guided Kylie to the kitchen table. "After she's eaten and rested, I'm sure she'll tell us all about where she's been."

Brooke just stared as Jill's eyes began to clear. Matt was right. Kylie still looked dazed and hardly capable of holding a coherent conversation.

"I'll get her something to eat." Jill tugged at Brooke's arm, annoyed that Brooke stayed planted where she was. A few minutes later, Jill set a muffin and a glass of milk in front of Kylie, who had yet to speak.

Jill tugged on Brooke's sleeve and nodded toward the door. "Come on, Brooke. Matt will take care of Kylie. I need to get to work, and you're going to be late for class."

Brooke looked at Jill, then back at Kylie and Matt. Shaking her head, she gathered her books and let Jill escort her outside.

Once they were alone, Matt sat next to Kylie. He watched her halfheartedly pick at her breakfast, barely aware of his presence. All of the eloquent proposals he had been mulling over in his mind vanished, and he found himself pulling the newly purchased engagement ring out of his pocket.

"I'm sure you have a logical explanation about where you've been," Matt began.

"Uh-huh," Kylie mumbled.

"And I know you would have called if you could have." His voice was calm even though his hands were shaking.

"Mm-hmm."

Matt stood and paced across the room. "I thought they had relocated you again," he said as much to himself as to her. "I can't go through losing you again." He turned, and she glanced up at him, her eyes still glazed.

Kneeling down next to her chair, he flipped open the box that housed the diamond solitaire ring. "Will you marry me? I don't want the FBI to be able to separate us again."

Kylie nodded weakly, staring blindly as he slipped the ring onto her finger. "Makes sense," she mumbled as he took her into his arms.

"I love you." Matt brushed his lips across hers and pulled her close.

Kylie responded automatically, her voice raspy from lack of sleep. "I love you too."

"Come on." Matt pulled her toward the living room. "You should lie down for a while. You need rest."

She lay down on the couch, snuggling into a throw pillow as Matt tossed an afghan over her.

"I'll call you later." Matt kissed her as her eyes fluttered closed. She was already sound asleep by the time he stepped out of her apartment.

* * *

The afternoon sun streamed into the apartment as Kylie struggled to push back her dreams in order to find reality. Images of the past week jumbled together. The trial. Those endless minutes in the car as gunfire had sounded around her. The three-day investigation to determine how her route had been compromised. The never-ending hours that had stretched into days in the car. Being passed from one agent to another until Doug had finally appeared to bring her the rest of the way home. And somewhere in there, she vaguely remembered a dream when Matt had proposed marriage. Or at least she remembered him slipping a ring on her finger. Surely, her brush with death had caused her to imagine that Matt, too, wanted to get married sooner than later.

She sat up, shaking her head as she became fully awake. She could hardly discern what was dream and what was reality anymore. Taking in her surroundings, she wondered how she had ended up on the couch in her apartment.

"Must have been Doug," Kylie muttered, stretching her arms over her head. She rose and walked into the kitchen, trying to remember when she last slept in a bed. Three nights ago? Four?

She heard the front door open, followed by her roommates' voices. They rushed into the kitchen as she pulled a glass from the cabinet.

"Are you awake now?" Jill asked as she placed her purse on a kitchen chair.

Brooke joined her. "Where have you been for the past week?"

"I'm sorry I didn't call." Kylie turned to face them. "My grand-mother passed away."

"Oh, I'm so sorry." Jill crossed the kitchen and embraced Kylie.

Kylie just nodded. "We knew it was coming. She had been sick for a long time."

"We were just so worried about you," Brooke told her.

"I thought that Doug had called and told you before we left for the funeral. I didn't realize he hadn't until we were on our way back."

"Matt said it was probably something like that."

Kylie pulled the milk from the refrigerator. "I need to call him and tell him I'm back."

Jill and Brooke exchanged looks as Kylie poured her milk.

"He saw you this morning."

Milk splashed onto the counter. Kylie turned to face them, her face pale. "What?"

"Don't you remember talking to us this morning?" Brooke asked, concerned.

Confused, Kylie shook her head.

Jill grabbed a dishcloth and started wiping up the spill. "You got milk all over you."

Kylie glanced down at the glass she still held and nearly fell over when she noticed the sparkle coming from her ring finger. Jill saw it at the same time, grabbing her hand for inspection.

"You're engaged!" Jill held her hand up as Brooke rushed over to see the ring settled on Kylie's left hand.

Kylie stared for a moment at the simple yet elegant diamond ring.

"When did that happen?" Jill asked.

"You just barely got back." Brooke reached for Kylie's hand, lifting it so she could get a better look at the ring.

Kylie shook her head, confused. She looked from one roommate to the other, unable to formulate a response.

"Well, let me be the first to congratulate you," Brooke continued, still studying the ring. "I knew you two were meant for each other."

"We're so happy for you," Jill said with a genuine smile.

Vague images of Matt played through Kylie's mind, mixing with the terror she had felt just days before. "No. That couldn't have been real." She fingered the ring with her right hand. "I was dreaming."

"Must have been some proposal!"

Kylie shook her head. "I heard all of you talking." She paced across the kitchen. "Then he said something about not wanting to lose me again, and he put a ring on my finger."

Jill and Brooke both watched her struggle to bring the memory forward.

"I must have been totally out of it."

"Do you at least remember saying yes?" Brooke asked anxiously.

Kylie shook her head as she tried to recall the vague memory. "I don't remember what I said."

Jill stepped into Kylie's path, forcing her to stop pacing. "The real question is, do you love him?"

"Yeah," Kylie answered without hesitation.

"So you do want to marry him," Brooke stated confidently.

Kylie looked from one roommate to another. "It isn't always that easy."

CHAPTER 18

His hair still damp from his shower, Matt picked up the phone. He was halfway through dialing the number when the doorbell rang. He opened it and pulled Kylie into his arms before she had time to react. "I was just about to call you."

"Can I come in?" Kylie asked hesitantly.

"Yeah, yeah. Come on in." Matt took her by the hand and pulled her inside, shutting the door behind him. "Kylie, what happened last week?"

Avoiding his eyes, Kylie looked down at their joined hands, Matt's ring still on her finger. "I'm afraid I wasn't exactly coherent this morning when you came over."

"Yeah. You did look exhausted," Matt agreed, leading her to the kitchen. "I'm so glad you're okay. Let me get you something to drink." Her recent absence made him realize even more that he could not live without her, now or ever.

Kylie just watched as he pulled the refrigerator door open and took out two bottled waters. She took the one he offered her, setting it down on the counter instead of opening it. "It was more like I was still half asleep."

Matt nodded and took a sip of his water.

With a sigh, Kylie took the ring off her finger and held it up. "What I'm trying to say is that I don't exactly remember how I ended up with this."

Matt blinked hard once and then shrugged. "We both said we loved each other and decided to get married."

"Just like that." Kylie stared at him for a moment, wishing she could remember more. "Did you actually *ask* me if I would marry you?"

Matt stepped closer to her and took the ring from her. Taking her left hand, he knelt down. "If I recall correctly, I was down on my knees, telling you how I can't live without you." Matt's eyes sparkled mischievously. "And that if you married me, your friends at the FBI wouldn't be able to take you away from me again."

Kylie tried to keep a serious face, but it wasn't easy with Matt kneeling at her feet, her hand in his. "And exactly what did I say?"

"Makes sense."

"Excuse me?" Kylie's eyes widened.

"You said that it made sense." Matt rose from his knees, his eyes searching hers. "What do you say now, Kylie? Will you marry me?"

Kylie took a deep breath and answered his question with one of her own. "What about your family?"

"What about them?"

"If you marry me, you could lose them," Kylie said softly. "And your chance to play baseball."

"I know."

Kylie thought of those long minutes outside of the courthouse, remembering how she had thought of Matt when she thought those minutes might very well be her last. She took a deep breath and pushed those memories aside, instead forcing herself to think logically. "Matt, I can't ask you to give up your family and your career for me. If we wait until after I'm out of protective custody, you'll know what you're getting yourself into."

"I know what I'm getting myself into now." Matt stared down at her and kissed her softly. "I want to marry you. I want to know that we can spend the rest of eternity together. Nothing else is more important than that."

"And your family?"

"Will understand and support my decision." Matt held the ring up.

Kylie reached up and stroked his cheek even as fear rolled her stomach. He was offering her everything she wanted—the knowledge that they could be sealed forever. Still, she worried about his safety as well as what he might be giving up. "Matt, you've made a name for yourself here. Even if you weren't a senator's son, you couldn't possibly get married without the press getting wind of it." She dropped her hand and stepped away from him. "We would be announcing where I am."

"Then we'll elope."

"Elope to the temple?" Kylie turned back to face him, eyes wide.

"Why not?" Matt shrugged. "The only people I really care about being there are my parents. I'm sure they could take an unscheduled vacation to whatever temple we choose."

Kylie nodded at the ring. "And our friends here? Jill and Brooke already saw the ring."

"Tell them you returned the ring and that we decided to slow things down for a while." Matt slipped the ring into his pocket and took her hands in his. "We can keep our marriage a secret."

"You want to marry me and then pretend we aren't married?"

"I want to be sealed to you forever. I'm willing to do whatever it takes to keep Rush's men from finding you." Matt pulled her closer. "Kylie, we can work out the details. The real question is, do you want to spend the rest of eternity with me?"

"Matt, I do love you, and nothing would make me happier than to be your wife," Kylie began. Panic threatened as she pushed aside her needs and wants and brought forward her logical side. Still, she forced out the words, "I just don't know that now is the right time for us to make this decision. I need time to think about this."

"How much time do you need?" Matt took her hand and lifted it to his lips. "I want you to feel good about this too. Perhaps we should pray together about this."

Kylie hesitated a moment. "No, Matt. I need to get my own answer."

Matt dropped his shoulders as he let go of Kylie's hand and drew her into an embrace. After a few moments in silence, Kylie pulled herself from Matt's arms.

"Why don't you go get us some food," Kylie began. "That'll give me a few minutes alone to think about things. I know I want to marry you, but I need to figure out if now is the right time to do it. There are so many obstacles, so many dangers."

"Will that be enough time?"

"I don't know, but it's a start," Kylie answered.

"If that's what you want." Matt grabbed his keys from the counter and headed for the door, Kylie walking beside him. He turned and gave her a soft kiss. "I'll be back in a little bit."

After closing the door behind Matt, Kylie turned to see the sketch of herself on the wall. She walked over to it, marveling again at Matt's skills. Most impressive was his ability to capture her inner self in his work, the parts she tried to hide from others.

Turning, she saw Matt's scriptures sitting on the couch. She crossed over to them and sat down. So many questions flooded her mind. Picking up his scriptures, Kylie began flipping through them, randomly reading bits here and there. A sense of peace began to fill her, and she could see the possibilities filling her mind. An urgency possessed her as her desire to enter the temple with Matt overshadowed all else. She didn't know how it would all work out, but she felt a quiet reassurance calming her, letting her know that it would. Silently, she slipped to the floor and began to offer a prayer of gratitude to her Heavenly Father.

* * *

"You did what?" Brooke shook Kylie by the shoulders, hoping to rattle some sense into her.

Jill dropped onto the couch in disbelief, staring at her roommates. Her soft voice penetrated through Brooke's shouts. "Brooke, let her sit down so she can tell us what happened."

Brooke dropped her hands to her side, but instead of sitting, she paced.

Kylie sat next to Jill and looked from one roommate to the other. "You guys, it isn't like Matt and I broke up. We just decided we need to take more time to get to know each other before we talk about marriage."

"But you're in love with each other!" Brooke threw her hands up in frustration.

Kylie took a deep breath. She wanted so much to share her plans with her roommates, but she couldn't put them in jeopardy. "Matt and I both know we want to be married in the temple. We need to know that our love is strong enough to last an eternity before we rush into such a big decision."

"I guess that does make sense." Jill laid her hand gently on Kylie's arm. "You two really haven't known each other for that long."

Kylie reached over and hugged Jill. "Thanks for understanding."

"Well, I don't understand." Brooke shook her head.

"Are you trying to get rid of me or something?" Kylie asked light-heartedly.

Brooke shook her head, a smile forming on her mouth. "Don't think I'm going to let you and Matt take things too slowly. Some things are just meant to be."

Before Kylie could respond, the doorbell rang.

"I'll get it." Brooke opened the door, surprised to see Doug standing on the other side.

"I just wanted to stop by and check on Kylie," Doug told her. He followed Brooke inside, but his eyes swept past Kylie and landed on Jill.

"I didn't think you were still in town," Jill said, suddenly uncomfortable after the difficult week of worrying about both him and Kylie.

Doug crossed the room and took Jill's hand. "I wanted to apologize for not calling you last week." He glanced at Kylie and then looked back at Jill. "I guess Kylie told you what happened."

Jill nodded, motioning for him to sit down. "I'm sorry about your grandmother."

Doug just nodded.

Kylie stepped forward and looked apologetically at her roommates. "I really need to talk to Doug. Would you mind giving us a few minutes alone?"

"I need to go to the library anyway." Brooke picked up her purse. "Jill, did you want to come too?"

"No, that's okay." Jill stood and stepped toward the hall. "I'll just be in my room."

Before she could disappear down the hall, Doug asked, "Jill, can I take you to dinner tonight?"

Jill's face flushed as she nodded. "I'd like that."

As soon as Jill's door closed, Doug looked to Kylie. "What's going on?"

"I just need to talk to you about a few things." Kylie took a deep breath. "Something happened a while ago I should have told you about . . ."

The doorbell rang before she could continue. With a sigh, Kylie stood. "Let me get that."

Doug leaned forward on the couch as he watched her open the door. His eyes widened as Matt Whitmore crossed the threshold and kissed Kylie. Doug jumped to his feet.

"What are you doing here?" he demanded.

Matt looked down at Kylie apologetically. "I guess you haven't told him yet."

"Told me what?" Doug's voice rose, his eyes darkening with anger. "How did you find her?"

"Can we sit down?" Matt motioned to the couch.

"I want answers, and I want them now." Doug stepped closer to Matt until there was only a foot of space between them. Impatience and fury were evident in his expression. "Just your presence here puts both of your lives in danger," he hissed.

"What do you want to do?" Matt's temper flared, even as he tried to keep his voice calm. "Are you going to kill her off again because we moved to the same town?"

"If you found her, then they can find her." Doug's voice vibrated with fury. "You know that Rush's men want nothing more than to see her dead."

"I know what they are capable of. I still have the scar to prove it," Matt reminded him. He took a deep breath, trying to control his temper. "Besides, I didn't find her. We ran into each other. It was completely coincidental."

Kylie placed a hand on each of their arms. "Doug, I depend on you to keep me alive, but Matt is the man I'm going to marry."

Doug's gaze shifted from Matt to Kylie, his eyes narrowing. "You can't seriously . . ." His voice trailed off when he sensed movement behind him. Jill stood at the end of the hallway, wide-eyed.

Her face was pale, and she stared at the two men who appeared to be preparing to do battle in the middle of the room. "I . . . I'm sorry. I just forgot to ask . . ." Her voice cracked as tears threatened.

Doug crossed the room quickly, putting his arms around Jill in an effort to comfort her. He berated himself for even having this conversation in Kylie's apartment, especially when there was anyone home. His anger abated as he quickly tried to assess the damage he had just caused to Kylie's cover.

Matt stared at Doug and Jill in disbelief. He turned to Kylie. "Is there something you forgot to tell me?"

"Doug started dating Jill when he dropped in on us a few weeks ago." Kylie held up a hand as she read the concern on Matt's face. "I didn't mention it because I didn't want to worry you."

Doug guided Jill to the couch and coaxed her to sit down. Sitting next to her, he looked intently into her eyes. "How long were you standing there?"

Kylie knew the answer just by the look on Jill's face. "She knows enough, Doug. You might as well trust her and tell her the rest."

Doug turned to Kylie. "First you and Matt tell me why he's here."

Kylie nodded, sitting on the floor. Matt sat in the chair behind her, resting his hand on her shoulder.

"Matt graduated early from college and signed on to play minor league baseball for the team here in town."

Doug looked from Kylie to Matt. Sarcasm laced his voice when he asked, "You didn't know she was here?"

Matt shook his head. "I saw her the first time at a church activity." He paused for effect. "A swimming party."

"All of our friends here think that we just met a couple of months ago. Brooke and Jill were even trying to get us together."

"You already knew each other?" Jill managed.

Matt smiled at her. "We were already in love with each other."

Jill looked from Matt to Kylie, confused. "But Kylie wouldn't even go out with you at first."

"I was afraid that if we were together, I would have to give up my life here," Kylie explained. "You and Brooke have been like sisters to me."

Doug leaned forward, resting his elbows on his knees. He rubbed his hands restlessly over his face before looking up at them again.

"Do your parents know she's here?"

Matt nodded. "They saw her on opening day. I didn't know they were coming."

"And they haven't told anyone," Doug stated, knowing the senator understood what was at stake.

"I still don't understand . . ." Jill looked from Doug to Kylie.

Doug took her hand in his. "Kylie is in the Witness Protection Program. I'm the agent assigned to protect her."

"Agent?"

"FBI. I've been with the Bureau for six years."

"But I thought you worked with computers," Jill managed to say, obviously confused.

"That's just an easy thing to tell people. I can't go around telling Kylie's friends that I'm FBI, or I might raise suspicions."

"And Matt?" Jill asked.

Kylie spoke now. "Before I came here, I was living under another identity. That's when I met Matt and we fell in love."

"The men after Kylie found her, so we moved her here," Doug finished for her. "Jill, you cannot repeat any of this. The men after Kylie will stop at nothing to find her." He paused until her eyes met his. "They will stop at nothing to kill her."

Jill's face paled at his words. She looked over to Kylie, seeing the truth of Doug's words in her eyes. Finally, she managed to find her voice. "What about Brooke?"

"She doesn't need to know," Doug told her.

Jill nodded, the color slowly coming back into her cheeks. As her mind began to clear, she turned to Kylie and asked, "Did I hear you say you're getting married?"

Kylie nodded, unable to suppress a grin. "As soon as Doug can help us arrange it." She reached up and squeezed Matt's hand, which still rested on her shoulder.

"Do you have any idea how complicated that would be?" Doug rubbed his face again.

"It gets worse, Doug." Matt grinned. "We're getting married in the temple."

"Mormons," Doug muttered, shaking his head.

CHAPTER 19

Finals. Swim practice. Baseball games. Kylie wondered how she even managed to breathe without scheduling it in. She had barely managed to get back in town in time to take her final exams. Though Doug had offered to give her a death certificate for her fictional grandmother so that she could postpone her exams, Kylie just wanted to get them over with.

Rarely did Matt have a day without a game, though Kylie had only managed to attend one since returning home. Still, they made a point of speaking on the phone every day. Matt frequently dropped by on his lunch break between practices, often working out in the gym with Kylie.

The frantic days Jill and Brooke had spent worrying about Kylie faded into memory as Brooke also focused on final exams and Jill prepared for the standardized testing her students were about to undergo. Kylie had hoped talking with Matt about the latest attempt on her life would help put it behind her, but nothing she did helped erase the memories of those bullets sounding so close to her. Her dreams were haunted by the sound of the shattering glass, the ring of the bullet hitting the car.

Her attempts to block the memory proved futile, and each discussion with Matt brought that day forward when she realized how much she wanted to be sealed to him. The urgency she felt to get married overwhelmed her at times, and she tried not to think that she might not live to marry him if they waited until after the trial.

If Matt noticed the tension that had settled on Kylie's shoulders, he kept the observation to himself. His one attempt at talking to her about the trial had upset her to the point of tears, and he had not tried bringing it up again. To everyone around them, Matt and Kylie's relationship was casual, and debates were not uncommon about whether they were dating or just friends.

Kylie pushed open the door of her apartment, sunshine raining in behind her. "I am so glad that's over." She dropped her book bag onto the couch, breathing a sigh of relief.

"Speak for yourself." Brooke glared at her from behind a text-book. "I still have two more finals today."

"Sorry, Brooke." Kylie flopped onto a chair. "Is there anything I can do to help?"

Brooke just shook her head in frustration. "Jill already quizzed me." She closed her book and slid it into her backpack. "I guess I'd better get this over with. Wish me luck."

"Good luck," Kylie said, watching Brooke gather her things and leave the apartment. She pushed aside a little pang of guilt as she thought of how much she was now keeping from Brooke.

Throughout the week, Jill had become a huge asset in under-mining the seriousness of Matt and Kylie's relationship. She success-fully planted the right comments in front of the right people to start the rumor mill among the young single adults. Already, several girls in the stake were making appearances at his games, trying to win favor to become his next girlfriend.

Kylie wandered into the kitchen to raid the refrigerator. She was finishing her yogurt when Jill walked in.

"Did Brooke already leave?"

Kylie nodded, licking her spoon clean. She opened the refriger-ator, searching for something else to eat.

"Well, what's happening with the wedding plans?" Jill asked anxiously. "I haven't had a chance to talk to you alone all week."

"Doug is supposed to be working on getting Matt's parents out here." Kylie pulled ham and cheese out of the refrigerator. "The bigger problem is getting my temple recommend without anyone getting suspicious."

"You can trust the bishop."

Kylie nodded as she fixed a sandwich. "I know, but Doug wants me to get my recommend from another bishop since I want to stay here after I get married."

"How are you going to do that?" Jill asked. "I thought you didn't want anyone to know you're getting married."

"Matt will keep his apartment, and I'll keep living here." Kylie shrugged. She rolled her shoulders in an attempt to relieve the stiffness that had settled there. "Everyone will think that we're just dating. Or with your help, they'll think we're just friends."

The doorbell interrupted their conversation. "That must be Doug," Kylie said as she carried her sandwich with her to the door.

The exasperated look on Doug's face made Kylie hold back a grin. "Come on in." As soon as Kylie shut the door, she added, "Brooke already left."

"How am I supposed to get you your temple recommend without blowing your cover?" Doug seemed anxious and frustrated.

Kylie sat down, motioning for Doug to do the same. "There has to be a way."

Jill came in and sat next to Doug. "Problems?"

"This religion of yours is causing me way too many sleepless nights," Doug grumbled.

A look passed between Jill and Kylie before Kylie spoke. "Is that because of my wedding plans or because of the Book of Mormon Jill gave you?"

Doug hesitated to admit that it was passages from the Book of Mormon that were keeping him up at night.

"Maybe it's time you got down on your knees and asked the Lord if these things we've told you are true," Jill suggested.

"What about this temple recommend thing?" Doug evaded her comment by changing the subject.

"I don't suppose there are any FBI agents who also happen to be bishops?" Kylie asked hopefully.

Doug shook his head. "I don't know of any FBI agents who are even Mormon."

"Then you haven't looked very hard," Kylie stated simply.

"What am I supposed to do, go around the Bureau and ask everyone what religion they are?"

Jill shook her head. "I doubt it's that complicated. You probably already know some agents who are Mormon—you just don't realize it."

"Can't you think of anyone you've worked with who doesn't drink coffee or alcoholic beverages?" Kylie asked.

"I do remember this one guy I worked with a couple of years ago." Doug shook his head, trying to bring the memory back. "We were on a stakeout, and he was drinking hot chocolate instead of coffee. Everyone teased him about it."

"He might be LDS." Kylie stretched her legs out in front of her. "If he is, he should have an idea of how to help me."

"I guess I can make a couple of calls . . ." Doug said hesitantly.

"In the meantime, why don't you come to the game with us tonight?" Kylie suggested. "We have an extra ticket since Brooke can't go."

"I don't like the idea of you going to Matt's games."

"And it would look strange to my friends if I didn't," Kylie told him. "Matt doesn't talk to me at the games, and if we go out afterward, we always just meet somewhere."

"Still . . ."

"Come on, Doug." Jill stood up and reached for Doug's hand. "You can come with us and evaluate the situation." She grinned and winked at Kylie.

Doug let Jill take his hand, and he stood next to her. "I thought you were on my side."

* * *

Lying on the bed in his hotel room, Doug studied the tape of the day's game. He was both pleased and surprised that Kylie had been correct. Apparently, the general public did not know Matt Whitmore had a girlfriend.

Several times during the locally televised game, the cameras had zoomed in on girlfriends and family members of the more popular players on the team, but Kylie had remained an anonymous face in the crowd. With Matt's celebrity status continuing to grow, Doug assumed that the television crews would have singled out Kylie had they known about her.

The section where they sat had been filled with Matt's friends. Doug could pick them out even before the introductions were made.

Each of them had something about them that made them different from the rest of the crowd. He couldn't quite put his finger on what it was, but he found himself drawn to the way they all accepted each other so easily.

Ever thorough, Doug watched the evening news. The sports highlights didn't offer anything of interest, but the story on the upcoming educational summit in Dallas had him sitting up straighter. As the anchorwoman described some of the expected guest speakers at the summit, an idea began to form.

Retrieving his laptop computer, Doug sat down and got to work.

CHAPTER 20

The elementary school was situated peacefully on a quiet street, the front shaded by mature trees. The American flag flapped in the breeze, interrupting the silence. A moment later, the peaceful setting was transformed when the school bell rang and the side doors flew open. Little bodies began shoving their way through the doors to freedom. Friday. Voices raised as fresh-faced children made their way to the line of yellow school buses. Others exited through the front of the building to meet their awaiting rides.

Doug got out of his car, leaning on the hood while he waited. The noise level settled to a dull roar as the first busload of children departed. He turned back to look at the main entrance, smiling when he saw Jill step outside.

The wind teased her blonde hair into her eyes, and she pushed at it absently, shifting the large bag she carried over her shoulder. Her cotton dress hung to her ankles, the ties in the back accentuating her waist. She moved through the stream of children, often turning to speak to one as she passed. As another school bus pulled away from the curb, she lifted a hand to wave.

She turned then and saw him. Doug could see the change in her expression even across the crowded parking lot. Her eyes warmed, and her lips quirked with the beginnings of a smile. She hesitated at the curb, checking for traffic before crossing the parking lot to him.

"What are you doing here?"

"Looking for you." Doug's grin flashed. "My sister just had her baby this morning. I was hoping you might come with me to visit her at the hospital."

"I'm not sure your sister will be up to meeting anyone new today." Jill hesitated.

"Oh, come on." Doug took her hand. "I mentioned you might come with me, and she was excited about meeting you."

"Are you sure?"

Doug pulled open the passenger-side door. "You have to come. I don't think I can deal with the stories of labor and delivery without some serious emotional support."

Laughing, Jill slid her bag behind the passenger seat and got into his car. She wasn't sure where the butterflies in her stomach came from, but she did her best to ignore them as Doug started the engine.

Twenty minutes later, Doug led her into the maternity ward at the hospital. After stopping to check at the desk, they made their way down the hall to his sister's room. With Jill's hand in his, Doug led the way inside.

"So you decided to show up?" Doug's sister Alana smiled, and her gaze shifted from her brother to the woman beside him.

"You know me. I always show up for new babies and free meals." Doug released Jill's hand to cross to his sister. Leaning down, he kissed Alana's cheek and then pulled the baby blanket aside to catch a glimpse of the tiny bundle in her arms. "She's going to be gorgeous, just like her uncle."

Alana let her gaze fall back down to the newborn in her arms.

Jill stayed by the doorway, unsure whether to advance or retreat. The connection between brother and sister was so clear she could almost touch it. She found herself staring at Alana, surprised at how fresh she looked after just giving birth. Her raven hair fell past her shoulders, and her face was beautiful, even exotic, despite the lack of makeup. Glancing from Doug to his sister, Jill easily recognized their similarities.

Doug straightened and held his hand out to Jill so she would join him. "Jill, this is my sister Alana."

Alana smiled at her as she approached. "It's nice to meet you. Doug has told me a lot about you."

"It's nice to meet you." Jill smiled in return, peeking down at the sleeping infant. "Your baby is beautiful."

Alana turned her baby so that Jill could see her better. "Jill, I just have to ask you something."

Jill straightened at Alana's serious tone and the intense expression on her face.

"How did you end up with my brother here?" Alana chuckled and lifted a hand, absently waving toward Doug. "I mean, you look like an intelligent, sensible girl." She looked from Jill to Doug and back again. "A schoolteacher, right?"

"That's right."

"You're much too smart to end up with him." Alana grinned as Doug leaned down and twisted her nose.

"Don't listen to her." Doug pulled Jill closer, sliding an arm firmly around her shoulders. "She's just jealous that you'll be able to walk out of here today, and she's stuck eating hospital food until tomorrow."

Alana stuck her tongue out in a purely childish gesture. "If you really loved me, you would smuggle some decent food in for me to eat."

Jill relaxed against Doug, now enjoying the exchange between him and his sister. Deciding that any new mother should be granted such an easy request, she stepped away from Doug. "Alana, you just tell Doug what you want for dinner, and he'll go out and get it."

Doug looked down at her, surprised.

"Don't look at me like that." Jill kept her eyes on Doug and motioned to Alana. "She just gave birth. The least you can do is go get her a decent meal."

Alana laughed. "I like her."

"I did too—until today," Doug grumbled.

Five minutes later, he found himself heading out of the hospital by himself in search of a bacon double cheeseburger and chocolate ice cream. When he returned, Alana's room was crowded with family. His mother was arranging bouquets of flowers on the table next to the bed, chatting with Alana. Jill sat in a rocking chair near the door, his niece snuggled into her arms. His father was leaning over her shoulder, looking down at his newest grandchild with awe.

Doug contented himself to observe for the moment, watching from the doorway. Jill smiled at his father, chatting amiably as though they had known each other for years rather than minutes. A moment later, the baby began to fuss. Jill patted her back, standing to cross to Alana. Doug watched how Jill handled the infant so gently and capably. He could easily picture her with a child of her own, knowing that she would make a wonderful mother. His heart did one slow roll in his chest as he watched the exchange between Jill and his family. She belonged here. Even though he knew her beliefs were very different from those of his family, somehow she fit in.

Alana noticed him first. Or rather she noticed the scent of her bacon double cheeseburger. Doug tried to clear his mind and heart as he entered and passed off the food to his sister. Yet as he interacted with his family, he became even more unsettled with how perfectly Jill adapted to those most important to him.

* * *

The danger of their situation was becoming more apparent to Kylie. The urgency to get married was now overshadowed by a sense of panic. Kylie made her way to her seat in the stands, finding that she was unusually alone. Matt's friends from church were noticeably absent since it was an afternoon game and they all worked.

Sitting down, Kylie leaned back, taking in the perfect day. The sun was still high in the cloudless blue sky. A gentle breeze teased at the ends of her hair, and she brushed a stray lock away from her face. She was supposed to be relaxing today, but she couldn't seem to shake the tension in her shoulders.

A popcorn vendor passed by, and Kylie raised her hand to get his attention. She exchanged dollar bills for the generously buttered popcorn, turning her attention to the field as the away team jogged onto it.

She watched the game, barely aware when Matt strode up to the plate. He struck out, which only added to her bad mood. The teams traded places, Matt jogging out to his new position at second base. Kylie tried to stay interested in the game, but her mind kept wandering.

In less than two weeks, she and Matt would be married. She had no idea what her wedding dress would look like. She would have no bridesmaids. The only attendees for the temple ceremony would be Matt's parents and Jill. All of the things that most brides spent days, even months, planning, she would go without.

Jill had brought home a bridal magazine just the week before, smuggling it in for her to see when Brooke was out. It had only served to further depress her. She wouldn't have a wedding cake or a bridal bouquet. She hadn't needed to order wedding announcements or worry about scheduling a reception hall. Even their honeymoon would only be a night together at a hotel in Dallas. Matt would leave for a road trip just twenty-four hours after their wedding. Upon his return four days later, Kylie would once again have to pretend that Matt was nothing more to her than a casual friend.

Her stomach sank. She wanted more, so much more, than a secret marriage. Even as that thought crossed her mind, guilt sank in. She knew she had so much to be grateful for. Three times the Lord had protected her life against incredible odds. The man she loved was back in her life and wanted her to be his eternal companion.

Matt stepped up to the plate again, and Kylie watched him go to work. She knew he too was sacrificing a great deal to marry her. Instead of having a wife he could come home to each night, he would be settling for the snatches of time they could steal together.

Matt shifted his weight as a fastball was thrown, connecting to send it flying into the gap in center field. The crowd cheered, Matt slid into second, and Kylie tried to shake off her bad mood.

Hours later, Kylie leaned on the hood of Matt's car, an ice cream cone in hand. The ice cream parlor was crowded inside, and Matt now stood across from her in the corner of the parking lot.

"You're quiet tonight," Matt interrupted her thoughts. "Is something wrong?"

Kylie nodded, letting out a frustrated sigh. "I feel like I have this weight with me wherever I go." She lifted her shoulders and let them fall. "I think about next weekend and I get excited and frustrated all at the same time."

"It's just wedding jitters."

"No, Matt." Kylie shook her head, trying to find the words. "It's more than that."

"You aren't trying to back out on me, are you?" His voice was light, but his eyes showed a flash of concern.

Kylie shook her head, discarding her half-eaten ice cream cone into a nearby trash can. "I don't know what's wrong. I just can't shake this feeling."

"What can I do to help?"

"Just hold me." Kylie stepped into his waiting arms, sighing as her head settled on his shoulder.

They stood silently for a moment, Matt resting his chin on the top of her head.

Finally, Matt broke the silence, his voice barely louder than a whisper. "I know this won't be the wedding of your dreams, but I'll do everything I can to make you happy."

Kylie pulled back, looking up until his gaze met hers. Could he really read her thoughts so easily? Did he, too, regret that their friends and most of his family would not be able to share their happiness and joy on their wedding day?

She spoke now, taking care to choose her words. "Matt, you're everything I want. I just wish we could be a normal couple for our wedding day. Maybe it sounds selfish, but I want the world to know how much I love you and that I am lucky enough to marry my best friend."

"I'm the lucky one." Matt ran a finger down her cheek and lowered his mouth to hers. The kiss was meant to soothe, to comfort. Yet when he drew back, the tension was still there.

CHAPTER 21

Jill sat in the third row of the chapel with Doug by her side. Matt and Kylie were seated in the row in front of them with Brooke and Caitlin.

The opening prayer had already been offered, and the bishop now stood at the podium, introducing the speaker for tonight's young single adult fireside, Senator James Whitmore. As Senator Whitmore stood and took his place at the podium, several members of the congregation looked around until they found Matt.

Senator Whitmore spoke eloquently at the fireside that had been arranged specifically around his visit to Dallas for the educational summit. As he closed his talk, Jim bore his testimony. His words were simple as he spoke of his love and appreciation for his older Brother, Jesus Christ. When he bore testimony of the truthfulness of the restored gospel, his eyes scanned the congregation until they met Doug's.

Doug felt the warmth of the Spirit even though he wanted to deny it. Without even looking at those sitting with him, he had little doubt that they too felt moved by the senator's words.

Refreshments were served after the fireside, another custom Doug felt he could get used to. He expected that no member of this religion would ever go hungry. With Jill next to him, Doug stood to the side of the crowd, waiting for the chance to talk to the senator alone.

As the crowd thinned out, Brooke approached them. "I'm going to take off. Did you need a ride home?"

Jill looked to Doug, who shook his head. "I'll bring her home."

"Okay." Brooke glanced over at Matt and Kylie. "I'll leave the light on for you."

Brooke left with the last of the crowd, leaving only Matt and his parents, Kylie, Jill, and Doug in the cultural hall. Only the bishop and one of his counselors still remained in the building, and they were behind closed doors in the bishop's office.

Jim Whitmore approached Doug as soon as the room had cleared. "I have to admit that I was surprised to see you here tonight."

"I believe your son has something he wants to tell you." Doug motioned to Matt, who now stood next to his parents.

"Mom, Dad, Kylie and I are getting married Saturday."

"What?" Jim's eyes widened as he looked from Matt to Kylie to Doug.

Beside him, Katherine's face paled as she slid an arm around her husband's waist. Jim responded instinctively, lifting his hand to her shoulder while still keeping his eyes on Doug.

Matt had faced the unity his parents represented too many times not to recognize the concern. As though mirroring his parents, Matt slipped his arm around Kylie and drew her to his side. "I know this is unexpected," Matt began. He looked from his father to his mother, pausing before speaking again. "But we've prayed about this, and we know that this is the right thing to do and the right time to do it."

"Oh, honey." Katherine closed the distance and threw her arms around Matt, and then moved on to embrace Kylie. "We just want you to be happy."

"And safe," Jim added, his posture remaining more reserved than his wife's. He looked from his son to Doug. "What will this mean for Matt?"

Doug proceeded to explain their plans to the Whitmores—how they hoped to let Matt and Kylie remain where they were; their plans to keep their marriage a secret until Rush was convicted. Doug explained the possibility of Matt entering protective custody and the plans to avoid it. Schedules were discussed and finalized before everyone went their separate ways.

On the drive back to Jill's apartment, Doug was unusually quiet. Absently, his fingers drummed on the steering wheel as he mentally replayed the words spoken at the fireside.

Jill's voice broke into his thoughts. "What are you so serious about tonight? Is something bothering you?"

"Everything's bothering me lately," Doug admitted before he thought to censor his feelings.

"Pull over up here." Jill pointed to the small park on the side of the road.

He did as she asked, and when she got out of the car, he followed suit. Jill linked her hand with his and started walking down the dimly lit path. The breeze ruffled through her short hair, flipping the ends around her face.

"Tell me about it," Jill said softly. "Tell me what's bothering you."

"I don't know," Doug answered, trying to avoid discussing his feelings.

Stopping, she turned toward him. "Try telling me the truth. It won't hurt you."

In her heels, she was only an inch shorter than him, and he found himself looking into her eyes, trusting what he saw there. "I've been reading that book you gave me."

"And?"

"Look, it's been a lot of years since I went to church." Doug pulled his hand from hers and paced away from her. "Mom took me every Christmas and Easter, but that was about it."

"Does it scare you that this book is true?"

"I think it scares me that your religion is true."

"Why?" Jill looked at him with genuine concern in her voice.

Doug stared at her face, the sincerity and understanding radiating from her eyes, and realized he would rather be facing an armed criminal than having this discussion with her. He had recognized her innate kindness the first time he met her, and quickly afterward, he had noticed her brilliant mind as well. For weeks now, he had tried to ignore the depth of the beauty that radiated from so deeply within her.

Stepping forward, he brushed one hand along her cheek. His eyes darkened as he spoke. "You scare me. If I admit all of this is true, I will know how to find that intangible thing everyone is searching for. But what if I'm just not good enough or worthy enough to have it? What if I fail?"

"How do you know you won't succeed?" Jill asked simply. "Do you doubt Kylie and Matt will be happy?"

He wanted to deny it, but instead he just shook his head.

Jill continued, "They are willing to live apart and pretend they aren't even married because they love each other so much. Why are you afraid to allow yourself that kind of happiness?"

Doug shook his head. "I don't know."

"Maybe it's time you prayed about it," Jill suggested and turned toward the car, blissfully unaware of the evil entering the city.

CHAPTER 22

As she worked through her set of individual medleys, Kylie's mind wandered. Just one more day until she and Matt would be sealed for eternity. Doug, with Jill's help, had arranged for Kylie's temple recommend as well as Matt's recommend for their sealing. The agent Doug had remembered from years past had indeed been LDS and had turned out to be a stake president. With his help, receiving their recommends had been no different than for any other couple planning to get married in the temple.

The weekend before, Kylie had gone to the temple to receive her endowment with Jill at her side to help guide her through. Matt had been there as well, though he had arrived just moments before the session to ensure that a connection would not be made between them. The serenity she had felt as she entered the temple that day had been so incredible, and she finally entertained the hope that she could find peace in her future.

Kylie tried to picture herself kneeling in the temple across the altar from Matt. Of course, she couldn't visualize her dress, as she would have to borrow one from the temple. The stake president had assured her that the temple workers would be eager to accommodate her.

When Kylie's hand met with the wall, she stopped and glanced at the pace clock. To her surprise, her coach stopped her before she began her next swim.

"You will never guess who is here!" Ryan spoke excitedly.

Pulling her goggles off, Kylie shrugged, instinctively scanning the pool area. "Who?"

"Tom Harris. He's an assistant coach for Stanford University." Ryan glanced back over his shoulder. "He does most of their scouting."

Kylie's heart leaped into her throat as she forced her gaze to the man on the far side of the pool. Mr. Harris had been the man who had attended the state championships in Arizona and offered her a scholarship to Stanford.

Her heart raced as the man looked back at her. She knew instantly that this man was an impostor. She told herself that they couldn't have found her again, even as she knew they had. The man on deck was definitely not the same man she had met during high school. Hesitantly, Kylie asked, "Is that him?"

Ryan nodded his head eagerly. "Come on. I'll introduce you."

"Why is he here?" Kylie asked. Her voice remained calm despite her urge to flee.

"I sent in some of your training tapes to the coach for the next Olympics. I guess they must have been impressed if they forwarded them on to Stanford."

"You sent in videotapes of me?" Kylie choked out the words. She dropped back into the water down to her shoulders. Her mind whirled, and dread weighed heavily in her stomach. "Let me go freshen up. I'll be out in a minute."

Leaving her swim cap on, Kylie climbed out of the pool and slipped into the locker room. She quickly opened her locker, grabbed her swim bag, and raced to the other locker room entrance. Cautiously, she cracked open the door.

Her heart sank when she spotted the two men wearing dark suits with subtle bulges under their arms. She had been around Doug long enough to spot a shoulder holster under a suit jacket.

Quietly, she let the door close and raced back to the entrance to the pool. Peeking out, she saw not only the man posing as Mr. Harris, but two other men in street clothes.

Alone in the locker room, Kylie dropped her bag onto a bench and pulled out her cellular phone. Her hands shook as she dialed, and a sigh of relief escaped when Doug answered on the second ring.

"They've found me," Kylie told him, foregoing any courtesies.

"Where are you?" Doug clicked into cop mode instantly.

"I'm in the locker room at the pool. They have me surrounded. There are two in the lobby and three in the pool area. I don't know how many might be in the parking lot." Kylie stood to pace the locker room. "I bought a couple of minutes by telling my coach I was going to freshen up. One of them claims to be a scout from Stanford, but it isn't him."

"I'm five minutes away. You have to buy a little more time."

Kylie leaned her hands on the counter, staring at herself in the mirror. "I don't know how. Coach will likely send someone in to look for me in a few minutes." Even as she looked in the mirror, she noticed the reflection of the fire extinguisher behind her. "I think I have an idea."

"I hope so," Doug muttered.

Kylie examined the area by the fire extinguisher, looking for a fire alarm. Anxiously, she continued to scout for one, finally locating it next to the door to the lobby. "I'm going to set off the fire alarm. Maybe I can slip out during the confusion."

"No, stay where you are," Doug told her, a plan forming in his own mind. "How much more time do you think you have?"

"A minute, maybe two," Kylie whispered. She closed her eyes and thought of Matt. She was about to lose him again.

"Wait one minute, then set off the alarm. Then I want you to hide in the locker room. Stay in there, and I'll come get you."

"Okay." Kylie picked up her swim bag and stuffed it back into her locker. "But I want you to send someone to make sure Matt is okay."

"I'll send an agent over to keep it low profile," Doug agreed. "I'll see you in a few minutes."

"Make it fast, Doug." Kylie's voice wavered. "I'm counting on you."

"I'll be there."

Sixty seconds later, Kylie pulled the lever down and started the confusion that she hoped would save her life. Her whole body shook as she quickly tucked herself behind a partially drawn shower curtain in the handicapped shower stall. Crouching on the seat, she plastered herself up against the wall to keep herself hidden. She hoped if Rush's men came in looking for her, they would see the shower was empty and keep on going.

A moment later, the door came crashing open, and she heard men's voices inside the women's locker room. She tried to keep her breathing slow and quiet as the men began their search. With a prayer in her heart, she closed her eyes as the footsteps approached. The shower stall across from her was being searched when a new set of voices entered the locker room.

"What are you men doing in here? Everyone has to evacuate the building."

"We were just making sure the locker room was empty," a man's voice insisted.

"Everyone clear out." The fireman ushered them all out, and a few minutes later, Kylie heard Doug's voice.

"Kylie, where are you?"

She stood up so she could peek over the top of the shower curtain. When she saw that Doug was alone, she called to him. "Over here."

Outfitted in a firefighter's uniform, Doug approached her carrying a second uniform. "Put this on."

Kylie did as she was told, quickly slipping into the oversized uniform. Doug placed a helmet on her head and then led her out of the locker room. As soon as they emerged, two firefighters flanked them, and they all walked out of the building together. A moment later, Kylie found herself riding beside Doug in the fire chief's car.

"Is Matt okay?" Kylie asked, looking behind her at the confusion still reigning in the swimming pool parking lot.

"The agent I sent his way hasn't checked in." Doug glanced at the rearview mirror. "We should hear from him in a few minutes, but for now we need to get you secured."

Kylie glanced back again, numbly watching another identity disappear behind her.

* * *

Matt parked his car and headed to the clubhouse. His teammates were already sauntering in as well, laughing and joking along the way as they prepared for the night's game.

"Hey, Matt," Chuck Player, the starting catcher, called out to Matt as he approached the locker room. "Is everything okay?"

"Yeah." Matt looked at him curiously. "Why do you ask?"

Chuck shrugged. "Some guys were here earlier asking about you."

Matt felt sweat form on his brow. "What were they asking?"

"Personal stuff." Chuck opened the locker room door and led the way inside. "You know, like if you have a girlfriend, who you hang out with. That kind of thing."

"What did you tell them?"

He shrugged again. "Wasn't anything to tell."

"Thanks. I'll catch you later." Matt patted him on the back and stepped back out of the locker room.

He turned suddenly when a hand grasped his shoulder. "Matt Whitmore?"

"Who wants to know?" Matt's hand clutched instantly into a fist.

"Agent Toblin. FBI." The man flashed his identification, raising an eyebrow when Matt leaned closer to inspect it.

"Is something wrong?" Matt asked, surprised his voice was steady.

"Agent Valdez sent me to check on you. There has been an incident."

Matt's face paled. "What kind of incident?"

"I don't know exactly." Agent Toblin nodded to the man sitting in a car across the parking lot. "We know Kylie's cover has been compromised . . ."

Matt opened his mouth, unable to ask the unthinkable.

"As far as we know, she's fine," Toblin assured him.

"I've got to go see her." Matt started toward his car.

"She's not there." The words stopped Matt, and reluctantly he turned his attention back to the agent. "Have you noticed anyone unusual around today?"

"I haven't, but my teammates have," Matt admitted and then proceeded to relay the information Chuck had given him.

"Valdez is going to want us to check out your car and your apartment, but we won't want to do that right now or we might raise suspicions." Toblin nodded at the players heading into the clubhouse. "You should get in there. I'll send you word when we hear from Valdez."

"I can't go in there and just pretend everything is okay." Matt's eyes darkened as he looked at Toblin with disbelief.

"That's exactly what you're going to do." Toblin's voice took on a hard edge. "No one will suspect you know Kylie is here if you act normal now that she's missing."

"I don't know if I can." The muscle in Matt's jaw twitched as he managed to choke back his emotions.

"I promise I'll send word when we hear something."

Matt nodded, forcing himself to make his way back into the locker room. Mechanically, he went through the motions of warm-ups and preparations for the game, but his concentration was lacking, and he knew it.

Twenty minutes before game time, Matt saw Doug approaching the dugout with Paul Channing, the manager of the team. Matt tried to stay calm when Doug was introduced as a reporter from the *Washington Post*. A few minutes later, Matt was alone with Doug in the manager's office.

Doug turned to Matt. "First of all, Kylie's safe."

Matt dropped into a chair, relieved. "Where is she?"

"I can't tell you that. We can talk about details after the game. I just wanted you to know that she's okay."

"How did they find her?" Matt asked, afraid of the answer.

"It wasn't you. Her coach accidentally tipped someone off."

"I need to see her," Matt demanded.

"You have to play tonight," Doug insisted.

Matt shook his head. "I have to talk to her. I'm not going to just let her disappear out of my life over this!"

"If you play, Rush's men will have no reason to think you and Kylie are together. We apprehended three of the men who came after her, but we know there were more than that," Doug told him. He watched a number of expressions pass over Matt's face. "I can arrange for you and Kylie to meet on your next off day."

"I don't know if I can do this." Matt lowered his head into his hands. "What if I lead them back to her?"

"Trust me to take care of that," Doug insisted. "I can have an agent double for you so that it looks like you're still with your team. Even your coach won't know you're missing."

Matt raked a hand through his hair and stood to pace the room.

Doug went on to explain the plan to make sure Matt had not been compromised. After the game, a double would be sent in for him, someone who would look like Matt from a distance. His car would be towed as though it had broken down so it could be checked for explosives or any other tampering. Then Matt's double would go to his apartment and search for any evidence that Matt had been identified by Rush's organization.

Matt listened to the details, his own mind racing. He leaned his head back, closing his eyes as he let reality seep in. Just one day before his wedding, and Kylie was gone again. Their plan to keep their marriage a secret had already been weighing heavily on both of them, knowing that they wouldn't be able to lead a normal life for months to come, but at least they had had a plan. Now everything in life was uncertain again.

He lifted his hand and rubbed at the stiffness in his neck. Memories of the year he and Kylie had spent apart came flooding over him, and a lump formed in his throat as he thought of the complete isolation he had felt during that time. The uncertainty of what time and distance would do to their relationship was as big a fear as what would happen if Chris Rush found her. Now that she had been found again, would they have to live through that solitude once more? Even if they were kept apart physically, Matt doubted that he could survive the emotional separation again.

When Doug finished explaining the logistics of keeping him safe, Matt voiced the only real question on his mind. "What about our wedding?"

A sigh escaped Doug as he spoke. "You have a choice to make. We can put you under protective custody too, but that means no baseball, no family, no ties to the past until Rush is behind bars. Even then, we can't guarantee your safety if you leave the program."

Matt opened his mouth to agree, but he was overwhelmed with a sense of panic. He would sacrifice anything for Kylie, yet he couldn't voice the words. After a moment, he finally spoke. "It doesn't feel right for me to leave right now."

"Then we should postpone the wedding."

"No." Matt's answer was immediate and absolute, surprising himself as much as he surprised Doug. He needed to know that Kylie would continue to be an integral part of his life, despite the physical distance that would certainly be between them in the coming months.

"What?" Doug looked incredulous. "You know she can't stay in Texas, and it wouldn't look right for you to quit baseball with the success you've had. You could be separated for months, even a year or more."

"Doug, I know we're supposed to get married now." Matt thought of his parents, who were in the stands right now waiting to watch him play. He ran a hand through his hair. "I have to trust that the Lord will find a way for us to be together."

"I'll talk to Kylie. If she says the same thing, we will try to arrange it for your next off day." Doug hesitated before adding, "Your parents won't be able to be there. You can't tell them about it."

"I know," Matt whispered, wondering if Kylie would agree to go through with the wedding. He tried to think of what their lives would be like over the next year if they did manage to get married. Would he be able to visit her? Could they at least talk on the phone?

Doug moved to the door. "In the meantime, you have to go out there and play your best game. Don't let anyone suspect that anything is wrong."

Matt nodded, but he detoured to the locker room before joining his team. He knew this was one time he wouldn't be able to make it on his own. Next to his locker, he knelt in prayer, voicing his requests in a quiet voice. Tears threatened as he stood, and he brushed them away with the back of his hand. When he turned, he was surprised to see Doug standing by the door. Without a word, Doug turned and left the room.

CHAPTER 23

Jimmy Malloy glanced behind him for the second time in as many minutes before stepping into the crowded, dimly lit cafe. He took a moment to scan the restaurant, ignoring the lunch menu that was scrawled on a chalkboard behind the counter. Locating Leonard Abbott took all of three seconds. He already had his handkerchief out, dabbing at the sweat on his forehead.

Annoyed at the display of weakness, Jimmy turned to the cashier and ordered the special without even reading what it was. He pulled out his wallet, pleased to see that his hand was steady. He tried not to think of how close he had come to getting collared. He still wasn't quite sure how the girl had managed to get away again, but at least he had been smart enough to delegate the dirty work to his subordinates this time. He had been in the parking lot when the sirens had sounded. As soon as he saw the cops coming, Jimmy had done the one thing he had mastered over the years. He had gotten lost.

After exchanging cash for food, Jimmy crossed the restaurant to the booth where Leonard was now playing with the straw in his diet soda. He slid into the booth across from Leonard, looking much more casual than he felt. The note he passed to the nervous little man across from him would undoubtedly upset Chris Rush when he learned of its contents, but Jimmy knew that Rush's anger would work to his advantage. The price on Christal Jones's head would go up again, and he planned on being the first in line to collect. Next time, he would take care of her himself.

* * *

Doug parked in front of the church. Wearily he rubbed a hand over his face and leaned his head back in his seat. He had never faced those left behind before. Already he had spoken to Matt's parents. They had been in the stands waiting to watch the game when he managed to discreetly pull them aside.

Finding himself the bearer of bad news, he had informed them that the wedding they were in town for could no longer take place. Even more difficult than explaining the situation to them was withholding the information that their son still intended to marry Kylie. Not someday after Rush was convicted, but at the earliest opportunity. Doug knew he couldn't risk someone following the Whitmores to the wedding, which left him with little choice but to let them think that there would not be a wedding in the foreseeable future.

As the Whitmores had listened to Doug's explanation, their relief that Kylie was safe was quickly replaced with concern for their son. Doug could hardly blame them for worrying, but, as he had explained to Matt, the young man had to continue on as normal for them to keep him safe.

Now, Doug had to move on to the next phase. Kylie would be relocated, and he had to leave some kind of story with her roommates. First he would find Jill. He had an idea for a cover story, but he needed her help to make it work.

The youth dance Brooke and Jill were chaperoning had ended only minutes before, and teenagers were still streaming out into the parking lot. Laughter broke out as a group of girls rushed out the door. Doug watched them, envying their innocence and joyful exuberance.

For a moment he tried to picture Kylie as a young woman. She would have been so much like these girls, naive and carefree. He was certain that her solid faith in her religion would have been obvious even before her life had changed. A shudder ran through him as he thought of how close Kylie had come to losing her life today. Four times now she had escaped men who were notorious for destroying anyone in their way.

I don't believe in miracles, Doug reminded himself. Yet he knew that without a miracle, Kylie would not have survived the day, even with his help. He felt a warmth come over him, an understanding of sorts that he had never experienced before. With a shake of his head, Doug climbed out of his car and went in search of Jill.

Cleanup was well underway when he walked in the door. Adults and teenagers alike were working side by side, moving tables, stacking chairs, and vacuuming floors. Doug found Jill in the kitchen, up to her elbows in soapy water.

Warmth flooded him once again as he looked at her. She was so lovely. The curve of her cheek, the flawless skin, the dark, expressive eyes that sometimes hid under a fringe of bangs. Doug could see the perfection, yet her true beauty was so much more than what could be seen. He doubted she would ever fail to turn heads when she entered a room, yet she was so blissfully unaware of the effect she had on others, not only because of her beauty but also because of her innate kindness.

Before he managed to speak, Brooke interrupted his thoughts. "Hey, Doug." She slipped past him holding two trays of cookies. "Did you come to help us clean up?"

"It looks like I'm a little late for that," Doug said as Jill turned toward him.

Jill's smile was immediate. "I didn't expect to see you tonight."

"Can I give you a ride home?"

Jill nodded and gestured toward the garbage can. "Would you mind taking that trash out while I finish up here?"

"No problem." Doug hefted the two large bags of garbage and headed out back to the dumpster. By the time he returned, the parking lot was nearly empty, and he found Jill still in the kitchen. She was standing in the center of the floor, mop in hand. He stood there a moment, watching her as she hummed softly to herself.

Jill turned and saw him, a smile crossing her face. "I'm just about finished." She rinsed out the mop and efficiently slid the bucket toward the door with her foot.

"Where's Brooke?"

"She already left for home."

Doug simply nodded and waited for her to finish. Ten minutes later, the building was once again clean, and Doug led Jill outside to his car. He was still contemplating what to tell her when a car sped into the parking lot. Instinctively, he stepped in front of Jill before he recognized Brooke's car.

The car skidded to a stop, and Brooke leaped out of it. Her whole body was shaking and her breathing was labored.

Jill recognized the panic in her eyes and rushed over to her. "Brooke, what's wrong?"

"I don't know." Brooke shook her head. "I don't know."

"What happened?" Doug asked, his voice deceptively calm.

Brooke glanced around the parking lot and then let her gaze finally settle on Doug. "I went home, and when I parked, I had this funny feeling that something wasn't right." Brooke took a deep breath. "I just shook it off, and when I was walking up to our door, I got so scared."

"What did you see?" Doug asked.

"Nothing." Brooke shook her head. "I didn't see anything, but I could hear this voice telling me not to go inside. I just turned around and ran back to my car."

"It will be okay." Jill put an arm around her.

Brooke was trembling. "I was so scared."

Jill studied her roommate, and she too had an uneasy feeling. "Brooke, why don't we go inside. Maybe the bishop can give you a priesthood blessing."

Doug laid a hand on Jill's arm before she could lead Brooke inside. "I'll go check it out."

"Call the police first. I don't want you going there alone," Jill insisted.

"You're kidding, right?" Doug looked at Jill as though she had lost her mind. "Brooke didn't see anything unusual, and you want me to call for backup?"

Jill nodded. "Something isn't right, and I don't want you going in there alone. Just humor me, okay?"

With a sigh, Doug nodded. He thought of Rush's men who had evaded capture, yet he had stopped by Kylie's apartment himself not even two hours earlier to pack up some of her things. Even though logic insisted that they were overreacting, he could not deny the uneasy feeling he himself had felt as soon as Brooke had driven up. After calling the local police, he left Brooke and Jill behind to sit and wait.

Forty-five long minutes passed as they waited impatiently in the foyer. The bishop had given Brooke a blessing, yet a sense of unease remained. Finally, Doug returned, his eyes unreadable.

"Is everything okay?" Jill asked anxiously, skipping a greeting.

"What happened?" Brooke demanded.

"Your apartment was broken into. Whoever it was really tore up the place." Doug took Jill's hand and looked at Brooke. "I'm sorry."

Brooke just shook her head. "It isn't your fault."

"I don't want you going back there tonight," Doug insisted. "I already made reservations for you at my hotel. Tomorrow, I'll take you over to the apartment, and we can see if anything is missing."

"What about Kylie?" Brooke asked.

"I already called her. She's staying with one of our other cousins tonight," Doug improvised.

Within twenty minutes, Doug had both of them settled into their hotel room. He had hoped that they would take the separate rooms he had arranged for them, but Brooke was too uneasy to be left alone, so Jill insisted on sharing a room with her.

Doug flipped on the television when he entered his own room, annoyed that he had missed the news highlights. Toblin had already apprised him of the situation. Surprisingly, Matt had played well and appeared relatively at ease when a reporter approached him after the game.

With a glance at his watch, Doug realized that even now Matt should be trading places with his double and returning to his own apartment. Increased security and a secondary alarm system had been installed in the apartment to keep Matt safe. Doug knew he couldn't risk having an agent posted outside Matt's apartment for fear that Rush's men might notice.

The more immediate concern of implementing a cover story for Kylie's friends had Doug up and pacing the room. He had already decided that faking her death again would be too traumatic for her friends and would inevitably draw too much attention to the situation. Instead, he had decided on creating another family emergency. Since he had just used the excuse of her grandmother's death, he wasn't sure it would work again so quickly without Jill's help.

The image of Matt praying that afternoon came to mind. He knew Matt was religious, so much so that he had spent two years of his life serving a mission for his church in Venezuela. Doug had just never thought about a strong man like Matt praying. Certainly not the way he had that afternoon. Matt had looked almost broken when Doug had entered the locker room. Yet, as he expressed his willingness to put his fate into the Lord's hands, Doug could actually see Matt's strength increase, at least enough to go on with the charade to give him and Kylie the chance to be married.

Doug stood by the side of his bed a moment and then reluctantly dropped to his knees. He didn't know the words to say, but somehow he managed to begin as he had heard so many begin their prayers at various Mormon functions. "Heavenly Father, I know you have a lot to do and everything, but maybe you could help me find a way to help Kylie and Matt without hurting their friends. I know I probably shouldn't ask you to help me make their friends believe a lie about Kylie's disappearance, but I'm going to anyway. After all, I just don't want her friends to worry about her." Doug hesitated, wondering what he should say next. At a loss, he ended the prayer with a simple, "Amen."

He stood just as a knock came at the door. Habitually, he reached for his weapon and looked through the peephole. He dropped his hand from his shoulder holster and pulled open the door.

"Come on in." Doug gestured to the sitting area. "Have a seat."

Jill stepped inside and perched herself on the edge of the sofa. Her eyes were filled with concern, and tears were trying to surface. "Can you tell me what really happened?"

"Everybody is okay," Doug began. He took her hand in his and sat next to her. "The men after Kylie found her, but she got away, and we have her hidden."

A sigh escaped her, one of half relief and half distress. "I was so afraid something happened to her."

His fingers laced with hers. "She's going to be okay, but now I need your help to explain why she disappeared so suddenly from town."

Now Jill stood up to pace the room. She noticed the Book of Mormon on Doug's nightstand, pleased to see that it already looked well read. "Obviously that story about her grandmother's death wasn't true."

"No, it wasn't," Doug admitted. "I just needed a story to explain why she was late getting back home."

"Don't tell me she's going to have another death in the family." Jill grimaced at the thought.

"Actually, I was hoping you could help me out. I want you to spread around the story that Kylie's grandfather had a fall and broke his leg. Tell your friends that she's moving in with him for a while to take care of him."

"I don't ever remember you mentioning a grandfather." Jill tried to recall the conversations with both Kylie and Doug after their return. She and Brooke had been so relieved to see them both they had never bothered to ask for details about the grandmother or the family situation.

"The best cover stories stick with simple facts. Fewer details to mess up."

Jill mulled his suggestion over for a moment before speaking. "Since a lot of people know that her grandmother just passed away, it might seem plausible that she would go help out her family."

"I would think so, especially since she just finished final exams a couple weeks ago. Kylie isn't taking summer classes, so no one should be suspicious if she goes home for the summer. I'm sure most of the college students left for home right after exams," Doug stated, hoping that she would be willing to help him pass on the fabricated story. After all, it was for the greater good.

Just as Doug was doubting her willingness to help, Jill nodded. "I'll help you."

Doug stared at her in disbelief. Did Jill consent to help him because he prayed for it, or would she have helped anyway? He stared at her for a moment, considering. Pushing the question aside, he concentrated on details. "Do you think you can convince Brooke that Kylie left so suddenly?"

"She'll think it's strange if Kylie doesn't call or write."

Doug thought for a moment. "Right before we move her again, I can have her call." He sat back down on the couch. "I could probably have one of the agents out of Houston mail a couple of letters from her a week or two apart."

"Doug, it will all work out." Jill lifted a hand to his cheek and held it there when he turned to meet her gaze.

"How do you know?" His voice was low as his eyes searched hers for answers.

Jill brushed her lips against his, the tenderness of the gesture rocketing through him. Her voice was soft when she spoke, but they both knew her words were true. "Because it's supposed to."

CHAPTER 24

Kylie sat on the edge of the swimming pool, her legs dangling in the water. She continued staring out over the water as Doug pulled up a chair.

"I see you're working hard."

Kylie glanced up and then back at the pool. The tears didn't come anymore. Four days ago she was supposed to be married, and now she had no idea when she would see the man she loved again. The only good news she'd had since escaping from Texas was that Matt was safe.

Absently, she wondered where she would be located next, but she didn't care enough to ask. Her shoulders still ached from the miles she had swum over the past several days, trying to work out her frustrations. That pain was minor compared to the sore spots on her knees. She had never realized that it was possible to hurt so much from kneeling, but now she knew that even prayer could be painful.

Doug studied her a moment. For the first time, he saw true despair on her face. She rolled her shoulders to stretch them, more out of habit than to reduce the tension that had settled there. "Aren't you going to ask about Matt?"

"I got your message that he's safe." Kylie sighed softly. "That's all that is important."

"Is it?" Doug asked, pleased to see some life in her eyes.

"What do you want me to say?" Kylie asked flatly. "The trial date will keep getting pushed off until after the Olympic trials, and I have no idea when I will see Matt again. Rush has won. He's keeping me from everything that's important to me."

"Matt still wants to marry you." Doug waited for Kylie to lift her eyes to meet his. "In fact, he's hoping you will agree to marry him next week."

"You can't let him enter protective custody." Kylie's voice became passionate. The complacency that had surrounded her a moment before was gone, and now she stood to pace. "He loves baseball, and I don't want him to lose his family."

"I think he was willing to do both of those things, but he seems to agree with you that it isn't right." Doug paused until she turned back toward him. "He wants to get married on his next off day. We can have someone double for him while he's with you."

Kylie just stared, unable to speak as she absorbed his words.

"You would only have about thirty-six hours together . . ."

She dropped into the seat beside him, and Doug could almost hear the silent prayer going through her head before she nodded in agreement. Her voice lowered to a whisper. "When?"

"Tuesday."

Tears filled her eyes, gratitude mixed with apprehension. "Thank you."

* * *

"She got away." Leonard Abbott dabbed his handkerchief across his damp forehead.

Color flooded Chris Rush's normally composed features. The muscle in his jaw twitched as he pulled a chair from the table and sat. "How?"

"I didn't get all of the details," Leonard began. He took a deep breath before adding more bad news. "I understand that three of your associates were arrested."

"The time for subtlety is over." Rush steepled his hands in front of him, considering. He spoke in a deceptively calm voice, yet there was no mistaking the steely determination beneath. "I want her location, and I want it now. You are going to tell Malloy to use every available man. I don't want any more excuses. Even a cat only has nine lives."

Leonard nodded, grateful to withdraw from the cramped room. He tried to justify his involvement by classifying Rush's instructions as simply a message to be relayed between his client and his client's employee. Yet, deep down, he knew the hold Chris Rush had over him grew stronger with each meeting.

* * *

Right before dawn, the van from the cleaning service pulled up behind the hotel just a few miles from Temple Square. The only life visible in the alleyway was the homeless person sleeping at the entrance. No one had moved close enough to him to discern the earpiece in his left ear. The van parked, but no one opened a door. The "sleeping" figure spoke quietly into the transmitter at his wrist, giving the signal that it was all clear. A man dressed completely in black stepped out of the shadows, checking the alleyway twice before moving to the back of the van.

Two women stepped out first, unloading a cleaning cart and supplies. Matt followed, dressed in a plain blue janitor's uniform. He pulled a cart out with him as well and followed the women inside. They worked their way through the kitchen and then to the service elevator. When they arrived on the second floor, Matt handed over his cart to one of the women and then entered the stairwell. Doug was standing just inside the stairwell door. Holding a finger to his lips, Doug led him silently up several flights

Finally, on the ninth floor, Doug motioned for Matt to stop. He pulled a flashlight no larger than a ballpoint pen out of his pocket. Squatting down, Doug shined the light on the doorknob and slipped a thin magnetic card in between the door and the doorjamb. It took a moment for Matt to realize that Doug was fixing the door so that the security sensor would not register that it had been opened.

As soon as Doug had completed his task, he pulled open the stairwell door and motioned Matt into the hallway. Matt stepped through the door to find himself face-to-face with a man of similar height and build, dressed exactly like him. The man simply nodded to Matt and slipped into the stairwell as Doug entered the hallway.

Inside the room down the hall, Kylie paced anxiously. She had been living inside the system long enough to recognize the extra security measures and know that there was cause for concern. Whoever leaked her return route from her last court appearance had yet to be identified. Doug had not spoken to her about his suspicions, but she had noticed a number of new faces among the U.S. Marshals that now guarded her.

Her breath caught when the door opened and Matt stepped through. From behind him, Doug held up one finger before stepping back into the hall and closing the door.

Even as Kylie moved toward him, Matt crossed the room in three long strides, his arms wrapping around her. For a moment he just held her, breathing in her scent. Finally, he broke the silence. "I was so scared I wouldn't see you again."

Kylie pulled back enough to see his face. "Are you really sure about this?"

"Yes." Matt studied her a moment. "Are you?"

"I'm sorry about your parents." Tears formed in her eyes, and she blinked to keep them from falling. "I know you wanted them to be here."

Matt's hand caressed her cheek. "I guess we really are eloping to the temple. I imagine they'll be surprised when we find a way to tell them."

Her lips quirked into the beginnings of a smile. "I love you."

"I love you." Matt stroked her back as she snuggled her head against his chest.

He let his gaze take in the hotel room. It was a small suite, with a kitchen area combined with the living room. The doors to the bedroom and bathroom were on the far side of the room. His gaze landed on his luggage, which had been sent ahead several days before. The things he needed for himself were in the hanging bag draped over a chair. The suitcase next to it was there for an entirely different reason.

Matt linked his fingers with Kylie's and led her across the room. "Sit down. I have something for you."

"What?" Kylie sat on the couch, watching him as he lifted the suitcase and laid it on the coffee table.

"After the story aired on the news in Virginia that you had been killed, your old roommate brought me this." Matt flipped open the suitcase, revealing her clothing inside. He looked up to see the surprise in her eyes, quickly followed by hope. "I know you've replaced the clothes and everything, but I thought you would want this."

Kylie's eyes misted as he slid a manila envelope from beneath a stack of sweatshirts. He handed it to her, watching as she carefully drew out the photograph. Several minutes passed as she stared down at the photo, tears streaming down her cheeks. Finally she looked up and spoke. "Why didn't you tell me before that you had this?"

"I started to the first time you came to my apartment." Matt stood, then paced halfway across the room. He turned back toward her before he spoke again. Uncertainty showed in his eyes, and his voice was hoarse when he choked out the words. "I guess I was afraid I would find out that you loved Chase more than you loved me."

Kylie kept her eyes on his, searching for the right words. She reached a hand out to him, pleased when he took it and sat next to her. "I loved Chase. He was my best friend." She took a deep breath and continued, "Until I met you, I thought I might even be in love with him."

"And now?" Matt forced himself to ask.

"I know now that I loved him more as a friend. He was there for me when I needed him." Kylie lifted a hand to his cheek and brushed her lips softly against his. "You took his place as my best friend, but that's all. The love I feel for you is unlike anything I've ever felt before."

A sigh escaped him, and Matt closed his hand over hers where it still rested on his cheek. "Are you mad I didn't give this to you before?"

"We don't have enough time together to let little things bother us." Kylie smiled. "Besides, we need to get ready to go. We have less than an hour before we're leaving for the temple."

* * *

"What do you mean I can't go inside?" Doug turned to look in the backseat at Matt and Kylie.

"Just that." Matt shrugged. "Only members with current temple recommends can go beyond the lobby."

He glanced over at Agent Toblin, who was driving the car. Toblin just shrugged and fixed his gaze on the Salt Lake Temple, now only a few blocks away. Doug turned his gaze back to Kylie. "How am I supposed to protect you from out here?"

"Doug, the temple is the one place where I won't need protection." The words were barely out of her mouth when she saw it. She only caught a glimpse of the gun barrel as the dark van pulled up beside them, but a chill ran through her. "Get down," she shouted.

Doug turned just as the panel door of the van flew open. "Hit the brakes!" he shouted at Toblin as gunfire erupted. The driver's side windows shattered, glass raining everywhere. The car skidded abruptly as a bullet struck Toblin in the shoulder. Doug reached over and cranked the wheel, reaching with his foot to punch the accelerator. The wheels squealed as they crossed over to the other side of the street, heading back the way they came. Two cars they cut off swerved to miss them, slamming on brakes and honking horns. Behind them, metal collided, the sound vibrating through the broken window.

Even as the van made a U-turn to follow after them, Doug called out orders. "Kylie, call 9-1-1. See if you can find some cops to get this guy off us. Matt, see if you can help me switch places with Toblin."

Toblin was still conscious and, with Matt's help, was able to slide under Doug to the passenger side of the front seat. Doug settled into the driver's seat as Kylie rattled off their position to the local police. Sirens sounded just moments later, yet the van still closed in on them.

"How did they find us?" Kylie had no choice but to keep her head down since Matt had pulled her down to the floor and now shielded her body with his own.

"Shh." Matt rubbed her back, praying silently that they would survive the day. Glass fragments were embedded in his arms from when he had shielded Kylie from the shattered window.

A police car raced toward them, and Doug watched the van veer off onto a side street. The sirens wailed off into the distance as Doug glanced over at his partner. "How bad is it?"

"I'll live," Toblin muttered through clenched teeth. "Drop me off at a hospital and then go ditch this car. You've got to get her out of here."

Doug nodded, praying silently to find a hospital nearby. His prayers were answered when he saw the sign for the hospital just a block later. He slowed down enough to blend with the other traffic and then pulled up in front of the emergency room and parked next to an ambulance.

Two ambulance attendants were just coming out of the building, and Doug lifted a hand and yelled for them. "Hey, I've got a guy with a gunshot wound here. I need some help."

The men rushed over to the car, and once Doug had flashed his badge, they retrieved a stretcher and helped Toblin out of the car. Meanwhile, Kylie was picking glass fragments out of Matt's arm, grateful that he had only suffered some superficial cuts.

Minutes later they were back on the road. Doug headed for the airport, reserving airline tickets on the way. Yet, when he arrived at the airport, he pulled up in front of the rental car agency.

"You two go inside and rent a car using this ID." Doug handed an envelope to Kylie. "I'm going to go ditch the car and buy airline tickets to make it look like we flew out of here."

"Where should we meet you?" Matt asked as he forced open the car door.

"Pick a spot."

"The Jordan River Temple," Kylie suggested. "We'll meet you in the waiting room."

"You've got to be kidding me." Doug's eyes widened.

"It's only about thirty minutes from here." Kylie climbed out after Matt. "By then, I'm sure you'll have a plan."

With a reluctant nod, Doug pulled away while Matt and Kylie hurried inside. Kylie scanned her new ID, memorizing it quickly. She had Matt hang back when she approached the counter. Fifteen minutes later, they got into a blue compact car and started down the highway.

"I sure hope Doug's plan gets us into a sealing room sometime today," Matt commented as he navigated down I-15.

Kylie reached over and covered Matt's hand with her own. "He's gotten us this far. Hopefully, he'll let us get married at the Jordan River Temple."

CHAPTER 25

The early afternoon sun streamed through the rear window of the cab as Doug leaned back and let the day's events run through his mind. He was halfway to the Jordan River Temple before it hit him. He had prayed for help. It had almost been instinctive to ask for divine assistance when faced with danger. He shook his head as though it might help him clear his mind.

During all his years growing up—and even his six years with the Bureau—he could not remember a single time when he had prayed like that. Sure, he had asked for help occasionally when he got into a real bind—the "I'll be good from now on if you only give me what I want" kind of prayers. This had been completely different. The prayer had raced through his mind, and moments later it was answered.

He tried to push the thought aside as he reviewed the morning's events. Whoever had been feeding information to Rush had been working on this operation. The high level of security prevented those on this assignment from discussing the details with anyone, at work or otherwise. So someone had been very foolish or was getting paid a lot of money. Doug was betting on the money.

Mentally, he checked off those involved in getting Matt into the hotel that morning. That operation had gone smoothly, and he had handpicked those agents. In fact, they were the only members of the team that even knew of Matt's presence. Kylie had been so adamant about Matt's protection that Doug had fed a story to the perimeter teams that he was simply taking Kylie to the Church headquarters that morning to deal with the details for her next identity. Even Matt's parents had not been informed of the wedding for fear that they might alert someone to Matt's presence in Utah and lead the wrong people to Kylie.

Doug fingered the cell phone in his pocket, anticipating the moment when he would be free to make a call to his office. He ruled out the possibility that anyone in the Dallas office could be involved since he was the only agent who was aware of all of Kylie's movements—which meant that Rush had succeeded in recruiting someone with the U.S. Marshals.

From the airport, he had called the hospital to check on Toblin. He was relieved to find out that the wound was superficial and Toblin was unlikely to get more than a day or two off work for his trouble. He then called his office. Liz Fielder answered the phone and assured Doug that she would inform their superiors of the situation and continue to check on Toblin.

The temple dominated his vision as the cab neared its destination. The general shape of it was different than the Salt Lake Temple they had just tried to visit, as well as the Washington D.C. Temple he had seen daily when he had commuted from Maryland into the District years before. Despite the differences in architecture, though, Doug sensed their similarities—they all emanated majesty, peace, and serenity.

Doug paid the cab driver as he pulled to a stop in front of the temple. He barely even glanced at the denomination of the bill before he handed it over and leaped out of the cab. This temple was more simply constructed than the Salt Lake Temple, but the feeling of peace prevailed as Doug stepped inside. Standing inside the doors, chatting companionably with one of the temple matrons, were Kylie and Matt.

Matt noticed him first. He leaned over and whispered in Kylie's ear before crossing to Doug. He lowered his voice before speaking, nodding in Kylie's direction as he did so. "She thought we could get married here instead."

"I don't think that's such a good idea." Doug stopped speaking for a moment as a couple walked through the door and passed by them. "Someone had to have leaked where we were going to be this morning." Doug's voice was calm, belying the worry gnawing at his stomach. "A cab can be traced pretty easily, and I'm not so sure about the rental car."

The muscle in Matt's jaw twitched, and he glanced back over at Kylie. "We've been through too much to not be able to get married today, if not here then at one of the other temples close by."

"How many temples are in this state?"

"I lost count years ago."

"I sure hope we don't have to try them all," Doug muttered. He fingered the Swiss Army knife in his pocket. "Take this and go switch the license plate of the rental car with someone else's out there. Take them off a van or SUV."

"You want to steal someone's license plates while they're inside the temple?" Matt looked at him like he had lost his mind.

"We'll send them back," Doug told him. "Besides, if we put your plates on some big van or something, no one will even think to run the plates."

Matt nodded, stepping outside as Kylie crossed the lobby toward them.

"What is Matt doing?" Kylie asked, automatically lowering her voice.

"Switching the license plates on the rental car," Doug said with a shrug. "Can't be too careful."

"Are you going to tell me about your plan?" She hid her nervousness well, but Doug could see how hard she was struggling to keep it under the surface.

"After the car is ready, we're going to drive to another temple so you and Matt can get married."

Hope dawned in Kylie's eyes. "Which one?"

"Any one that's close," Doug said. A moment later, Matt pulled the rental car up in front of the building.

* * *

President Duncan hesitated at the door of his office. He was due at Church headquarters in an hour and a half, yet he couldn't shake the feeling that he had forgotten something. For nearly two years, he had been serving as the temple president in Provo. Those who knew him well recognized him for his organization, compassion, and often ridiculous sense of punctuality. Yet here he was, checking his desk once again for whatever was causing that nagging feeling that he was about to leave something incredibly important behind.

The phone rang and was ignored. When it rang again, he picked it up. "Hello?"

The temple worker from the front desk breathed a sigh of relief. "I am so glad you are still here. We have a couple who wish to see you. They say it's urgent."

"Well then. I guess you had better show them in." President Duncan settled behind his desk, and a few moments later, the door opened to reveal a striking young couple.

"I'm President Duncan." He stood, shaking hands with each of them.

"Matt Whitmore." Matt shook hands with him and nodded to the woman beside him. "And this is my fiancée, Kylie Ramsey."

President Duncan motioned for them to sit in the chairs facing his desk. "What can I do for you?"

Kylie took a deep breath and handed a large manila envelope to him. "We hope you can help us get married today." She explained the situation, offering only the most pertinent details. To his credit, the temple president listened calmly. He slid the contents from the envelope Kylie had given him, finding that the marriage license and temple recommends were in order. Additionally, a set of instructions was included, indicating that the marriage certificate would need to be hand carried to Church headquarters to be kept in a sealed file. The copy that would typically be given to the couple would be kept locked up by the FBI.

"I have to ask if you have prayed about your plans." The Spirit filled the room as President Duncan spoke.

Matt squeezed Kylie's hand as they both nodded. "We both know we're supposed to get married now. We are willing to trust in the Lord to help bring us back together."

"Do you feel the same way?" President Duncan asked Kylie.

Tears filled her eyes as she nodded once again.

"I certainly don't need to question your faith." He leaned his hands on his desk and stood. "I'll have someone show you where to get your clothing. Then I will perform the ceremony for you."

They were whisked away, and fifteen minutes later they were once again meeting with the temple president. The temple workers who helped Kylie had gone to great lengths to find a dress suitable for a wedding. Though it was simply cut, the white satin gown fit like it had been made for her.

The president explained the ceremony to them and then motioned for them to follow him. When he called Kylie by her given name, Christal, a thought occurred to Matt.

"What name am I supposed to call you by?" he asked before they left the office.

Kylie turned to him, also surprised to be called by her given name.

President Duncan looked from Matt to Kylie, slowly understanding the problem. "Brother Whitmore, have you ever called her by her given name?"

Matt shook his head.

Now Kylie spoke. "He will never be permitted to use my real name, not until I can leave protective custody. In fact, neither of us know yet what my next name will be."

"What about C. J.?"

"What?"

"It's your initials. C. J. for Christal Jones." President Duncan gave a shrug. "That way it still fits when this ordeal ends. I imagine the government can find some suitable first name that uses at least one of those initials."

Kylie smiled. "I think I like it."

"C. J. Whitmore." Matt nodded approvingly. "Come on. Let's make it official."

The two men who would witness the ceremony were already waiting in the sealing room. Though no words were said, both the bride and groom thought of Matt's parents and regretted that they couldn't be present. When they knelt across the altar, even that cloud dissipated, and the joyous event was as perfect as the start to any marriage could be.

CHAPTER 26

Matt leaned his head toward her, their foreheads touching. "I'm sorry we don't have more time."

"Me too." The hotel lobby was brightly lit despite the early morning hour. Two marshals led the way outside and began loading the car parked out front. In just a few hours, Matt would trade places with his double in time for his game in Las Vegas.

Running a finger down C. J.'s cheek, he wished fervently for more time. "Every night I'll be praying for us to be together soon."

"I'll be praying for the same thing."

Matt lowered his lips to hers, forcing himself to keep it light. "This is even harder than the last time."

"I know." C. J. stepped back, running her hands down his arms to link her hands with his. Both of their ring fingers remained bare to keep up the pretense that they were both still single. Tears glistened in C. J.'s eyes as she ran her thumb over Matt's hand. "I'll see you soon."

Matt nodded, unable to respond. He turned and stepped into the waiting car. A moment later, he disappeared.

* * *

The plan was simple enough. After tucking C. J. in a safe house with two agents that he knew he could trust, Doug flew to Dallas to start planting seeds. The money he expected to find was well hidden, but the list of possibilities was growing shorter with each incident.

Three times, information about C. J.'s travel plans had been compromised. Only two individuals had been assigned to all three trips. Doug studied the personnel files for both agents. Mark Lacey had been with the marshals for eight years, and his record was impeccable. In fact, his reputation was the reason he had been assigned to C. J. in the first place. Tara Baldino, on the other hand, had joined up only two years before.

Their efforts to track payments to any agents with access had been thorough, but no money trail had been discovered. Suspecting that the payoff may have been in cash, Doug spent the morning searching for overseas travel, safe-deposit box rentals, and even the bank accounts of family members. After hours of searching, Doug found what he was looking for. Tara Baldino had rented a safe-deposit box shortly after the first incident.

* * *

The first safe house was in the middle of nowhere. Based on the wide open spaces surrounding the small farm house, C. J. guessed it was in Wyoming. Only two FBI agents accompanied her, which left her nervous. Before, when she was changing identities, she was handed over to the U.S. Marshals. Yet, this time, only the two agents from Dallas were with her.

She had talked to Brooke a few days before the wedding, and she had written several letters that could be mailed from Houston for her. Now, after three days of doing little more than reading, boredom was beginning to set in. She had too much time on her hands, she thought. Too much time to think about Matt, to wonder about him. Just as she was considering how close the nearest swimming pool might be, Doug came rushing into the house. "We're moving out."

The urgency in his voice had her moving quickly, snatching up her purse and her duffel bag. C. J. had barely stood up when he grabbed her arm and pulled her out to the car. "What's wrong?"

"It's just a hunch, but I think we may have found the leak."

Within minutes, C. J. was alone in the car with Doug, speeding south into Colorado. They drove in silence for the first twenty minutes. As the distance between them and the safe house grew, Doug began to visibly relax.

"You think someone with the marshals is helping Rush." C. J.'s voice was matter-of-fact even though her hands were still shaking.

Doug nodded. "It's the only thing that makes sense. Your travel route has been compromised too many times for it to be coincidence."

"Where are we going?"

"There's a cabin in the mountains a couple hours outside of Denver." Doug spared her a quick glance. "You'll like it. It has a lap pool inside."

"Now you're talking." C. J. leaned back in her seat, forcing herself to relax.

Six hours later, Doug navigated his way through winding roads flanked by pine trees. The driveway he pulled into was more of a ditch than a road. It wound through the trees for a half mile before the cabin came into view.

Nestled in the trees, the cabin sprawled out as though fighting for every inch it could take from the forest. A front porch extended from the front door to wrap around the side of the cabin. On the second level, a common balcony followed the path of the porch below. The elements had faded the once-blue paint to a soft gray, and the small patch of garden in front was overgrown with weeds.

"Let's get you settled in." Doug pulled her single duffel bag from the trunk and led the way inside.

Though the garden outside was neglected, the inside was polished to a shine. The front door led directly into a large living area. Bowls filled with potpourri were arranged on end tables that flanked an oversized couch and two matching chairs. A fireplace dominated the far wall, next to which a wooden rack held a thick, handcrafted quilt.

On the other side of the front door, a glass door revealed a two-lane lap pool that stretched along the width of the cabin. A spiral staircase led to the bedrooms, but Doug ignored it and led the way to the back of the structure.

The kitchen was large, with a breakfast bar separating it from the generous kitchen table. Doug left C. J. there while he checked out the rest of the cabin. By the time he returned, C. J. already had a can of chili simmering on the stove.

"How long am I staying here?" C. J. gestured to the kitchen cabinets. "There's enough food here to make do for a couple weeks if you don't want anything with eggs or milk in it."

"The decoy route I sent the other team on will take a couple more hours." Doug glanced at his watch. "They should reach the other safe house after dark."

"Then what?"

"If all goes according to plan, we will arrest the mole and start prepping you for your new identity." Doug forced a smile. "Maybe we'll even go grocery shopping."

"Then I hope your plan works." C. J. spooned up two bowls of chili and rooted through the cabinets to find some crackers to go with it.

An hour later, the kitchen was cleaned up from dinner, and C. J. was already well into her first workout in days. Doug opened the door to the pool and walked inside unnoticed. He settled down in a lounge chair and loosened his tie as he watched her cut through the water.

He rested his elbows on his knees and stared out the huge windows across the room. The trees looked so peaceful in the last rays of sunlight. Yet, peace was still months away for C. J. and Matt, if not longer.

The only sound in the room was from C. J.'s continual motion through the water. Doug hung his head, not surprised to find himself praying silently that he could find a way to keep C. J. and Matt safe again.

His cell phone rang, disrupting the silence. "Valdez."

"It's Toblin. We just arrived at the alternate destination."

"Anything?"

"Nothing." Toblin's voice came through the line, clearly disappointed. "We leaked information to Lacey about the Rush case like you told us to, and Baldino was in on the transport so she had the information to pass on."

"The Rush case." Doug repeated slowly as memories came flooding back. "We always refer to C. J. as the Rush case."

"Yeah, so?"

"A while back Liz Fielder came into my office." Doug tried to focus on that seemingly insignificant conversation. "She asked me if I was working on the Jones case."

"Liz?"

"Toblin, she shouldn't have even known C. J.'s real name. She hasn't been in the office long enough."

"But she didn't have access to all three incidents." Toblin reminded him.

"Are you sure?" Doug thought back to the last trial. "I wasn't in the office for more than a week before C. J.'s last trial date. I can't be sure she didn't get into my files."

"I don't know . . ." Skepticism laced Toblin's voice.

"Think about it." Doug's voice grew more insistent. "Every incident happened after I had been away from the office for at least a few days. We all know how easy it is to pick locks on file cabinets if you have enough time."

"What do you want me to do?"

As Doug watched C. J. come to a stop at the far wall, he worked out his strategy.

CHAPTER 27

Katherine Whitmore stepped into the expansive living room in the large colonial home in Great Falls, Virginia. She stopped to look at the pictures on the mantel, her gaze going from her daughter Amy's graduation picture to the photos taken of Charlie as he prepared for his mission. Reaching out, she picked up a picture of Matt taken after he'd graduated from college the winter before.

As her children had grown, she had always prayed that they would stay strong in the gospel and someday find that special person with whom they'd want to go to the temple and spend the rest of eternity. Looking down at Matt's photo, she knew that there was so much more she needed to pray for now.

When Matt and Kylie had announced their plans to marry despite the threats against Kylie's life, Katherine had been understandably concerned for her son's safety. Now she was more concerned about his happiness. She and her husband had barely been able to talk to Matt before they left Texas to return home. Doug had kept them away from Matt while the extra security measures were being installed in his apartment. Then he had insisted that they keep their original airline reservations to avoid the appearance that anything was wrong.

Jim Whitmore found his wife in the living room clutching Matt's photograph. He crossed the room to her, dropping the mail he carried in his hand on the mantel. Putting his hand on Katherine's arm, he turned her toward him so she could find comfort in his embrace.

"Everything will work out for the best," Jim assured her.

"I just wish I could be there for Matt," Katherine told him. "I hate pretending that nothing is wrong."

"I know." Jim ran a hand down the length of her hair.

Katherine sighed deeply, glancing at the mail her husband had just brought in. "Is there anything from Matt in the mail?"

"I haven't looked through it yet."

Stepping away from her husband, Katherine lifted the stack and flipped past the bills and junk mail. She nearly dismissed the postcard from Las Vegas as junk mail until she caught a glimpse of Matt's handwriting on the back.

"It's from Matt." Katherine held the postcard so Jim could read it as well.

Mom & Dad,
Wish you were here. I finally got to the temple this week to finish up the work I had planned to do while you were in town.
Love, Matt

"They got married?" Katherine looked up at her husband incredulously.

"Let me see that." Jim took the postcard, reading it again. With a grin, he looked up at his wife, noticing the tears in her eyes. "I think they have just taken another step to prove that nothing is impossible."

* * *

Leonard Abbott dabbed the perspiration from his forehead with an already damp handkerchief. The humidity hung thick in the air, creating a haze over the nation's capital. Leonard walked along the sidewalk outside the Smithsonian Air and Space Museum. Despite the temperature, tourists were out in full force, cameras ready as people hurried to get out of the heat and into the air-conditioned buildings.

His own children were currently tucked away at the Natural History Museum with his wife. Public places, he thought again, should protect them from what he was about to do. Leonard heard the music from the carousel before he spotted it. He slowed his pace, mopping at his brow once again.

Nervously, he looked around at the children lined up to ride the brightly painted horses. He made his way to a nearby bench, trying unsuccessfully to look at ease. Less than a minute after he took his seat, a man sat next to him.

"Mr. Abbott," he said, continuing to look straight ahead. "I'm Doug Valdez."

"Can you protect us? Me and my family?"

"Yes," Doug answered confidently. "If you have something of value for us."

"Conspiracy to commit murder, extortion." Leonard swallowed hard. "I can help you keep the girl safe if you're willing to deal."

Doug nodded, and a moment later two U.S. Marshals were standing beside them. "We'll work something out."

* * *

Jill stood by her classroom door as her students exited for the last time. Several of the second graders hugged her as they left the room, and their voices in the hallway sounded giddy as they rushed for the doorway and their summer vacation that lay just beyond.

As the hallway emptied, Jill turned back to her classroom. She would have the rest of the week to put her classroom back in order and to make recommendations on the placement of her students for the next school year. She began removing the posters from the wall, each one serving to remind her students that learning was supposed to be fun. A movement from the doorway caused her to glance over her shoulder.

"Doug!" Jill crossed the room even as Doug moved toward her. His arms came around her, and she buried her face in his shoulder to hide her unexpected tears.

"Shhh." Doug ran a hand over her hair.

They just stood there for a moment in silence among the rows of child-size desks. Finally, Jill pulled back to look up at him.

"I wasn't sure I would see you again," she managed to say.

Doug leaned forward to touch his lips briefly to hers. "I'm sorry I haven't called. Things have been pretty hectic lately."

"Kylie?"

"She's fine," Doug assured her. "I need a favor, though."

Jill nodded automatically.

"Actually, I need two favors." He motioned for her to sit as he crossed to close the classroom door. He perched himself on the edge of the desk next to where she was sitting.

"What do you need?"

Doug took a deep breath and launched into the explanation he had gone over in his head so many times in the past few hours. He watched her eyes widen with surprise, then acceptance as he explained her part in his plan. She had no need to be informed about the other aspects of his plan that would be working simultaneously to help him prove that Liz Fielder was the person working for Rush.

Jill leaned back as she absorbed his words. "I understand what you want, but you said you need two favors. What's the second one?"

This time, Doug took her hand. "Will you wait for me?"

"Wait for what?" Jill looked down at their joined hands and back up at Doug.

"I want to get baptized," Doug forced himself to say the words, and now they began to tumble over one another. "I tried to convince myself that the gospel wasn't true, but I can't deny it anymore. I know I have to wait a year before I can go to the temple, so I'm asking if you will wait that year with me." Again he took a deep breath. "Next year, I want to take you to the temple and make you my wife."

Jill could only stare at him. In the back of her mind, she was grateful she was already sitting down or surely she would have fallen over from shock. All of her doubts and uncertainty about dating Doug suddenly seemed foolish. Her prayers that her relationship with him was somehow right had been answered time and time again. Yet she had been afraid to hope that he would find the truth that would allow them to be together.

"Okay, so you need some time to think about it." Doug's voice was now matter-of-fact as he reached for her other hand. He stood, pulling her up with him. Slowly, he slid his arms around her, and then without seeming to move at all, he closed the distance between them. His hand came up to caress her cheek and he lowered his lips to hers. The kiss was dizzying, and his heart slammed once, then twice in his chest. All of his thoughts were of Jill, of the promise a life together could hold. Slowly he drew back, searching her eyes as they began to clear.

"Well?" Doug rubbed his thumb over her lower lip. "Will you marry me?"

Jill's smile bloomed in contrast to the tears in her eyes. "Yes."

* * *

Reporters were already crowding around the players' entrance as Matt tried to leave the ballpark. He had noticed Jill in the stands that night, surprised to see that the rest of their friends were noticeably absent. He tried to make his way through the newspaper reporters to the parking lot, answering an occasional question only if he thought it would help him get to his car faster.

He had just gotten clear when Jill ran up to him and threw her arms around him. "You were great tonight!" she said loudly enough to have heads turning in their direction. She then lowered her voice so that only Matt could hear. "Just play along. It's important."

Smelling a story, several reporters shifted toward the young couple, cameras flashing as Jill continued to drape herself over Matt.

"I didn't think I would see you here tonight," Matt said cautiously, trying not to look bewildered as he followed Jill's lead.

Jill lifted her left hand to his cheek, the new diamond ring sparkling there for all of the cameras to see. "I wanted to surprise you."

"What's your name, honey?" one reporter shouted out as the cameras continued flashing.

"Oh, I'm Jill." She extended her right hand as though it was the natural thing to do.

The reporter shook her hand, launching into his next question. "Where did you two meet?"

"Why, at church, of course." Jill smiled for the cameras before turning to Matt. "You must be exhausted after such a long game." She turned back to the reporters. "Please excuse us."

Jill slid her arm through Matt's and steered him toward his car. She lowered her voice as she asked, "You will give me a ride home, won't you?"

"Only if you explain to me what that was back there."

Jill only nodded as Matt opened the passenger door and waited for her to get in.

Matt didn't say a word until they were well away from the stadium. "Okay, Jill. What's going on?"

"I'm sorry, Matt." Jill tried to hold back a grin as she noticed the blush rising in Matt's cheeks. "Doug tried to get in touch with you before the game, but you were already at the stadium."

"Well?"

"Doug thinks he knows who's leaking information about Kylie. He wasn't sure if they knew about you, so he wanted to make it look like you were involved with someone else."

"Don't you think the ring was overkill?" Matt nodded down at the engagement ring she wore.

"That was Doug's idea." Jill grinned as the excitement of her next bit of news caused her stomach to turn. "He wants you to baptize him this weekend."

"What?" Matt pulled over to the side of the road and slammed on the brakes. Now he turned to give her his full attention.

"We're getting married, and he wants to get baptized as soon as possible." Jill's smile lit up her face, and Matt's expression quickly mirrored hers.

"Has he even taken the discussions?"

"He was meeting with the missionaries tonight."

"Then congratulations." Matt leaned over to kiss her cheek before pulling back onto the road. He glanced down at the ring Jill wore, thinking of C. J.'s engagement ring, which was still hidden in his dresser drawer. *Everything will work out,* Matt reminded himself. *Just have faith.*

CHAPTER 28

C. J. stood on the balcony watching the fireworks in the distance as the locals combined with the summer visitors to celebrate Independence Day. She could hardly believe it was July already, as the cool mountain air reminded her more of early spring than the middle of summer. And after being locked up in the cabin for weeks on end, she certainly didn't feel independent.

She had been married a whole month now. That thought both pleased and depressed her. Knowing that she and Matt were sealed for time and all eternity gave her a comfort that she hadn't known would be possible. Yet the fact that they had not spoken since the day after their wedding was depressing beyond words.

Another splash of lights lit up the sky—a shower of yellow, then red, then green. Before all of the light had faded, a roman candle ignited, firing balls of color high into the sky. C. J. watched halfheartedly, wondering how long she would remain in Colorado.

Doug had disappeared several weeks before, leaving her with Agent Toblin. The sling and bandage that had helped his shoulder to heal had been discarded over a week ago, and he considered himself completely recovered from the incident in Salt Lake City. C. J. had questioned the fact that he was the only agent assigned to her at the moment, but he had evaded her questions. When Kylie tried persistence, Toblin simply ignored her.

News about Matt was nonexistent. She had thus far managed to keep herself occupied in the pool, the surrounding woods, and with the various reading materials Toblin continued to provide for her. She had even started working on some correspondence courses in an attempt to keep her mind occupied.

Though Toblin said little, she knew that Rush's inside man was still at large. Otherwise, she would have been relocated by now. She took advantage of having a pool in the house, practicing two or sometimes even three times a day. Still, she missed having a coach and people to train with. No matter how hard she tried, she knew that the Olympics would remain a dream unless Doug could help her find a new coach with the ability and experience to train a world-class athlete.

As another burst of fireworks lit up the dark sky, movement on the ground caught her eye. She shifted into the shadows of the balcony as two cars pulled up in the gravel driveway beneath her. Toblin stepped out onto the balcony next to her, his weapon in his hand. He held up a finger to his lips, though his eyes stayed on the cars below.

The headlights on both cars went off, then the lights on the car in front flashed two times. Toblin stepped forward on the balcony as three figures climbed out of each car and headed toward the cabin. A moment later, the cars both pulled away, leaving the men behind.

"What's going on?" C. J. whispered.

"Looks like Valdez is laying a trap." Toblin motioned for her to follow him inside.

"Here?"

Before Toblin could speak, Doug rushed up the stairs, taking them two at a time. "C. J., come with me."

She followed him into her bedroom as two women made their way upstairs. "What's going on?"

"I think I know who the mole is, and I'm afraid I won't have time to get you out of here safely." Doug circled the room, opened the closet door, and then checked the window. "One of the female agents will stay in here with you tonight, and I have two that are headed up to the roof right now with night-vision goggles."

Another burst of fireworks went off, and Doug grabbed C. J.'s arm, pushing her against the wall. Keeping his body pressed against the wall, Doug moved back to the window. Frustration laced his voice when he spoke again. "It's going to happen during the fireworks."

"What?" C. J. slid down the wall until she was sitting next to the dresser.

"The night-vision goggles won't work while the fireworks are going off. They'll blind my guys every time one shoots off." Doug stepped into the hall and signaled to Toblin. After giving him instructions, he moved back to C. J. "If I were coming for you, I would do it while the fireworks were going off. It would disguise the noise and it keeps us from seeing them coming."

"Now what?"

"Your prayers couldn't hurt." Doug motioned for her to follow him.

Staying low, she followed him into the hallway. From her view, she could see an agent posed just inside the front door, gun already drawn. A female agent stood at the top of the stairs, holding her weapon down at her side. Toblin stood to the side of the window in the upstairs loft. He held a hand up, which Doug mimicked. The hand signal passed from one agent to another, though it did not result in any action.

Seconds later, another burst of fireworks lit the sky, followed closely by gunshots. Doug put a hand on C. J.'s shoulder to keep her in place. The only way anyone could get into the hallway would be through Doug or Toblin.

Toblin pressed back against the wall as the window by him shattered. A second later, he crouched beside the broken window, firing his weapon out into the darkness. The noise was deafening. The sky lit up again, and this time the front door flew open. Three men burst through, running for cover even as more shots rang out. As though they could read each other's minds, Doug and the two agents covering the front door each downed one of the three men.

The gunfire stopped for a moment, and C. J. hoped that the ordeal was over. Then Doug turned, gun in hand, and fired at a figure standing behind her. C. J. gasped as a man fell at her feet.

Doug's eyes remained hard as he stepped on the man's hand that held the gun, relieving him of his weapon before confirming that the man no longer had a pulse. C. J. scooted away from the body as Doug lifted a walkie-talkie to his mouth. "Are we all clear?"

"Affirmative," a voice came back over the device.

"Do another sweep just to make sure," Doug ordered before turning to the woman on the stairs. "Riley, get our transport back here."

"You got it."

Doug holstered his weapon and reached a hand down to C. J. He felt her tremble even before she moved into his arms.

"It's okay." Doug held her, hoping his words were true.

* * *

Matt moved through the locker room to change out of his uniform. His pants were covered in mud from his slide into second base, and the front of his uniform sported stains from a diving catch he made in the eighth. The team had lost the game, despite Matt's home run in the fourth inning. As he passed the manager's office, he heard his name called.

"Good game tonight," Paul Channing began, motioning for Matt to come in and close the door.

"Thanks." Matt closed the door behind him. "What's up?"

"I just wanted to ask you, have you got a suit?"

"You know me. Of course I have a suit."

"Good. You'll be needing it tomorrow night."

"Tomorrow we're playing Oklahoma. Why would I need a suit?"

"We're playing Oklahoma tomorrow." Paul pointed at himself and then circled his hand to encompass the locker room. "You'll be playing in Philadelphia against the Padres."

Channing stood up and offered his hand. "You've been called up, son. Congratulations."

"I'm going to play for the Phillies?" Matt repeated even as he automatically shook his manager's hand.

"Their first baseman got injured last night. Out for the season," Channing told him. "Andy Muhler is the manager up there. I've known him for years. When he called and asked about you, I told him you could fill anyone's shoes. Don't make a liar out of me."

"No, sir!" Matt blinked at Channing, stunned.

"You had better get packed up." Channing handed an envelope to Matt. "Your flight leaves first thing in the morning."

With a nod, Matt left the room, his shock quickly turning to joy. He only wished, with an ache in his heart, that he could share it with his wife.

CHAPTER 29

"Hi, Liz." Doug leaned on the cubicle wall next to his own.

"Doug, I didn't realize you had returned." Liz leaned back, tapping a perfectly manicured nail on the arm of her chair.

He shrugged and held a file out to her. "Do you remember a while back when you offered to help on the Jones case?"

"Of course." Liz nodded, taking the file that he offered her. "What do you need?"

"Someone keeps leaking information about Jones's whereabouts." Doug lifted a finger, scratching his temple as though trying to figure something out. "I think it must be someone with the marshals."

"Do you have any leads?" Liz's voice remained businesslike, but her fingers were now fiddling with the edge of the file she held.

"A couple. I even planted a few phony routes, but nobody took the bait."

"Maybe someone tipped them off that Jones wasn't really there."

"I thought of that too." Doug nodded, appearing to agree with her. "Why don't you take a look at the file and see what you think."

She opened the file with a gasp. The black and white photo was grainy, but no one would doubt that it was Liz Fielder who was picking the lock of Doug's file cabinet. Instinctively, she looked up to the ceiling where the photo had obviously been taken from.

As though reading her mind, Doug spoke. "That's right." He lifted a finger, pointing to a light fixture above his cubicle. "We actually placed four cameras, but the one up there definitely got the best footage."

Two uniformed policemen appeared at Doug's side, and Doug spoke again. "I think these gentlemen have an appointment with you." He stepped back as one of the policemen pulled Liz to her feet and relieved her of her weapon. He didn't tell her that with Leonard Abbott's testimony, he had more than enough evidence to convict her. "Feel free to take the photos with you, Liz. I made plenty of copies."

* * *

"Philadelphia?" C. J. stared out the window as Doug drove her through the historic city. She wondered idly when she would find time to go see the Liberty Bell.

"That's right." Doug wove through the early morning traffic with ease.

C. J. sighed. "You know, I've been meaning to ask you something."

"What?" Doug noticed the uneasiness in her voice.

"Back at the cabin." C. J. clasped her hands together and then pulled them apart again. "How did you know that man was there? The one who came from the bedroom? I never even heard him, and he was right behind me, but you turned and shot him like you had been expecting him."

"I think we'll have to credit that one to divine intervention."

"Excuse me?" C. J.'s voice held both surprise and disbelief.

"We never really had time to talk when I first got to the cabin." Doug glanced over at her, a corner of his mouth quirking up. "I guess I never told you that I had Matt baptize me last week."

"What?"

"And Jill and I are getting married next year."

Stunned, C. J. just stared at him as he pulled up in front of a sleek high-rise. "Anything else you haven't told me about?"

"Jill thought you would want to know that Brooke's missionary is planning on coming back to Texas for school," Doug said. "And I mailed your last letter to her a few days ago to let her know you wouldn't be back."

"Anything else?" C. J. asked, amazed at how much had happened in Texas in her absence.

"We're here." Doug evaded her question, turning to her. "C. J., welcome to your new home."

Still stunned from Doug's news, C. J. pulled her duffel bag from the backseat and slung it over her shoulder. Doug gave her name to the doorman, and the middle-aged man nodded to her and opened the door.

Clad in jeans and a T-shirt, she felt like she was trespassing as she entered the elegant lobby. Vaguely, she wondered why she would be living in such an upscale building, but Doug's announcements were at the forefront of her mind. Doug led her to the elevator and pressed the button for the fourth floor. After they boarded, C. J. leaned against the side of the elevator, staring at him.

"When you see Jill, make sure you tell her congratulations for me."

"You can count on it." Doug stepped out of the elevator and led the way down the hall.

C. J. followed him to her door and watched him unlock it himself before handing her the keys. "Here you go."

"Thanks." She pushed the door open wider before turning back. "Aren't you coming in?"

He simply shook his head, nudged her inside, and closed the door between them.

C. J. just shook her head at Doug's odd behavior and then turned to look at her new home. She stood on the thick, pewter-colored carpet that flowed down a hallway on one side and into a spacious living area on the other. Cushions in shades of blue and gray were scattered over a pearl-colored plush couch. Flanking it were two chairs of smoky gray. A generous breakfast bar separated the living room from the kitchen, which boasted slate counters and gleaming white cabinets.

Stepping farther into the living room, she ran a finger absently over the polished coffee table. She lifted a throw pillow from the couch, hugging it to her chest as she stepped to the window to explore the view.

Matt watched her from the hallway, mesmerized by her simple movements. Her name tumbled from his lips, a whisper really, but she turned at the sound. He saw the expression on her face change from fear to disbelief to pure joy in the space of two heartbeats. The pillow she held dropped to the floor, and they moved toward one another. As tears filled his eyes, Matt knew that once again, their prayers had been answered. They were together, and they were home.

ABOUT THE AUTHOR

Traci Hunter Abramson is originally from Phoenix, Arizona. After graduating from BYU, Traci worked for the Central Intelligence Agency for six years before resigning to become a stay-at-home mom. *Ripple Effect* is her second novel.

Besides family activities, Traci enjoys reading, cooking, and swimming. She has also coached the North Stafford High School swim team for the past nine years.

Traci and her husband, Jonathan, currently live in Stafford, Virginia, where Traci serves as the stake Young Women's sports director. They are the parents of four children.